Secret

Devotion

The Lord's Sovereignty

Pursuit's Cure

Nelson P. Miller

Secret devotion—pursuit's cure.

Miller, Nelson P.

Published by:

Crown Management, LLC – August 2014

1527 Pineridge Drive
Grand Haven, MI 49417
USA

ISBN: 978-0-9905553-2-2

Images are from the Poplar Heights Farm research study of early memorial stone cutters in the latter half of the 19th century in western Missouri. See www.stone.poplarheightsfarm.org.

To Virginia, Anne, and Sarah

Crown and Scepter—The Lord's Authority

"I will give you riches stored in secret places."

Table of Contents

1

Arrival

"I am a foreigner and stranger among you."

The young woman—she might almost have been a girl—appeared in town without notice, town folk later recounted to one another. She had gone straight to the small window of the clerk's office in the old city hall at the high end of the town's main street. There she had asked about a room to rent for a short stay in town. *She found no room at the inn.* The city clerk had sent her to the ad board in the drugstore in the middle of town. The drugstore clerk had told her about a widow who rented rooms in the old mansion at the high end of main street back near the city hall. The widow had taken in the young woman. No one knew anything more. If the widow knew, then she was not saying, which would have been unlike her. She was usually a reliable source of interesting information about her infrequent short-term guests.

1

The young woman stayed longer than town folk had expected. Most often, travelers passing through kept their stays brief. The town had little to offer travelers or new residents. Years had passed since anyone had moved into town, while many, especially the young, had left. The town's aging population made more curious the young woman's lengthening stay. She had no reason to stay, at least not in any prospect for youthful relationship. She had no family or friend in town. No one knew her, and she knew no one. Yet she stayed. A few small cleaning jobs and caring for the town's elderly gave her the income to keep up her room in the widow's home. *She sought her God and worked wholeheartedly.* She took meals in the homes she cleaned or with the widow.

Lamb of God and Victory Banner

What little the town folk learned of the young woman, they liked. She had a bright way about her. Though none would admit it, the town's residents took silent encouragement from the sight of her slight figure moving back and forth through town attending to her duties. Her movements seemed to renew old acquaintances among the town's residents while at the same time kindling new connections. What was more, the young woman was outgoing and friendly with everyone, even the many town folk who were not friendly with her or one another. *A happy heart makes the face cheerful.* The town had a dour spirit to it, travelers knew. The young woman's presence made a slight change in that spirit, as encounters showed.

"Two, please," the young woman indicated with a nod of her head toward the rolls in the glass case. She smiled and blinked several times as she caught the baker's glance, her eyes twinkling.

"Aye, two is it?" the baker smiled back at the young woman, "One for you and one for that little friend you're hiding behind you?"

The baker pretended to look over the young woman's shoulder. She turned to see no one behind her. The baker chuckled at his game, the same one he had learned to play with the young woman every day she came to pick up rolls for herself and the widow.

"Now where did he go?" the young woman quipped playfully, "He was right here just a moment ago. He's probably back by your oven stealing one of those treats you're saving for yourself and your bride." *The city streets will fill with girls playing there.*

Another customer entered the shop as the baker and young woman completed the sale with more cheerful banter. Watching the young woman leave, the baker slowly turned to smile at the next customer.

"Oh, it's you, is it?" the baker grunted, his smile disappearing as he paused to reflect for a moment, but then adding, "Well, how can I help you, then?"

"How 'bout a few of them rolls?" The toothless customer pointed to the glass case. *I was hungry and you gave me something to eat.*

"How about you reach into that pocket of yours," the baker started but then stopped as he watched the customer wince and start to turn for the door.

"Hey, here, listen, never mind," the baker resumed. He used his big hand to scoop a handful of rolls into a little paper bag and reach across the glass case with it. Seeing the customer's hesitancy, the baker gave him a little nod and hint of a smile. *If your gift is mercy, do it cheerfully.*

The customer's eyes narrowed as if distrusting whether the baker could really be so generous. Yet he took a step back to catch the little bag in his hand while grunting, "On my tab then, please." The baker let the bag go without another word, watching the toothless customer leave quickly. The baker smiled, though, as he thought again of his banter with the young woman. *God loves a cheerful giver.*

The young woman returned to the widow's residence, where she and the widow enjoyed the baker's rolls over breakfast tea. She then headed down to the low end of the town's main street to sweep and dust at the dry goods store.

"Good day, Ma'am," the young woman greeted the elderly store owner behind the counter, "I've come to chase your mice again today."

"Aye, there's plenty of chasing to do, my lass," the owner smiled back at the young woman, who was already donning a dusty apron. The owner gazed longingly at her for a moment before adding more frankly than she wished, "You look so much like my daughter in that apron."

The young woman caught the reluctant sentiment in the owner's voice and eye. She hesitated a moment, then said as tenderly as she could manage, "Here, let me run these mice away again first. Then you tell me about her, will you?"

The owner smiled and nodded with glistening eyes.

Just then, a loud thumping came from the flat above the store. Scowling, the owner took a deep breath and turned toward the stair at the back of the store, ready to let out her habitual bellow at her disabled husband thumping his cane on the floor upstairs as his signal for help. Yet instead, she caught herself. *A cheerful heart is good medicine.* Walking quietly to the bottom of the stairs while the thumping continued, she lifted her head and said as gently as she could muster, "I'll be right up, Sweetheart."

The thumping stopped. The owner glanced back at the young woman, already hard at work with the broom. The young woman looked up at the owner. They smiled at one another. Then they simultaneously started to giggle and then to laugh. The thumping resumed. "Coming, dear. Coming dear," the owner called up the stairs, still giggling.

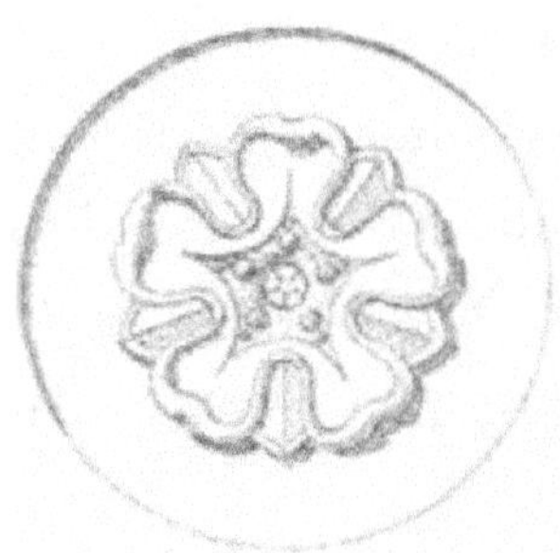

Messianic Hope and Promise

The young woman took her midday meal that day with the parson and his wife. *I was a stranger and you invited me in.* Folks in town still called him the parson, although it had been years, actually decades, since the town had an active church. The parson had never quite discerned what had happened to his ministry

5

work. It had faded away so slowly that no single event had caused him to take any notice. One day he ministered to an active flock, while the next day he ministered to no one. So it seemed, although the passage had in actuality taken many years.

With the town bereft of church life and the parson's spiritual instruction, the town's few shopkeepers served double duty maintaining the community's spirit. It is naturally so in small towns, which after all are largely the product of necessary commerce. Folks must have a place to purchase essential goods and services. The manner in which shopkeepers conduct their trade, whether honest or dishonest, generous or parsimonious, establishes the basic spirit of the town. *You must have honest weights and measures.* Religion usually leavens and elevates the mix. Without it, commerce alone had left this small town with its unusually hard-faced spirit.

With no income from any church work, the parson subsisted instead doing light carpentry jobs, fixing small things like broken gates and the odd piece of wobbly furniture. *Isn't this the carpenter?* He had no training as a carpenter and no strength or youth for heavy carpentry work. He had simply slowly acquired the carpenter's craft as he had worked alone over the years to maintain the town's one aging church. That church now stood derelict, boarded up.

Most of the parson's little carpentry work he now did in a makeshift shop in the lean-to behind the parsonage in which he and his wife continued to live. The parson's lean-to kept him near enough to care for his wife. The town's residents regarded the parson's wife as suffering from senility. *She pretended to be insane in their presence.* With this conclusion, the parson vehemently disagreed. He admitted only that his wife needed his company from time to time throughout the day. Indeed, he was glad of her need. He treated it less as need and more as her gracious willingness to desire him as a worthy companion. He knew that plenty of other husbands in the small town received no similar grace.

The parson still appreciated the young woman's willingness to sit with his wife while he attended to jobs that kept him away longer than the hour or so that his wife could usually spare him. *She stayed and worked with them.* This day was one of those days. The parson could not pay the young woman, but they would share with her one of his wife's outstanding home-cooked meals. In this way, the young woman learned more of the town's history including its spiritual decline that had left the parson to ply his carpentry.

"I must get going," the parson said to his wife, adding reassuringly, "You are in good hands, Dear."

The parson's wife looked away anxiously. Noticing, the young woman took her hand with a reassuring smile. The parson's wife looked at the young woman, mimicking if not yet fully returning her warm smile.

"Let's go clean up the kitchen," the young woman encouraged the parson's wife, who smiled more warmly this time and rose to clear the table. The parson slipped out quietly as the two women busied about the kitchen. Two hours later when the parson returned, his wife seemed oblivious to his ever having left. The parson breathed a sigh of relief, thanking the young woman, who slipped away unnoticed so as not to upset the parson's wife once again.

Happy events like these seemed to follow the young woman wherever she went about the small town. *The cheerful heart has a continual feast.* The only thing that the town folk found troubling about the young woman was that they could discover nothing significant about her past. *Past troubles will hide from my eyes.* All that she would share responding to their plying inquiries was the vague sense that she had left a stable home out of a sense of adventure. This explanation the town folk assumed to be false. No one would have chosen the town for adventure. If the young woman had not been so cheerful and well liked, then rumors would have become fact in the minds of the town's residents. The rumors included that she was an abused or neglected child, or had run from an undesired suitor, or had fled creditors. *A gossip separates close friends.*

As it was, none of the rumors took hold. The town's residents accepted the young woman's bona fides undoubtedly because of her constantly cheerful demeanor. The town's residents decided tacitly that she was welcome to stay as long as she wished without defamation's burden. Their accommodation was extraordinary. The town was not one in which newcomers got to keep secrets. Few secrets survived, and where they did survive, gossip of the worst kind ordinarily filled in the blanks. The young woman's most salutary initial effect on the town may have been that for the first time in a long time, it accepted a degree of privacy among one of its residents.

The only one who might have had a clearer view of the young woman's origins was the town's doctor. To call him the town's doctor is too generous to the town. The town was too small to have a doctor of its own. The doctor on whom its residents called came from a distant town, serving several small towns on a medical circuit of sorts. His wide travels enabled him to observe the movements of residents and travelers from town to town.

Indeed, like the lawyers who served the region's small towns in their own circuit duties, he knew much more about the reasons for those movements than any of the town folk knew. Yet the confidentiality that he owed his patients kept him from sharing or even entertaining any gossip. The town's residents knew that they could get nothing from him. *A trustworthy person keeps a secret.* So when he quietly dodged questions about the young woman, no one assumed that he knew anything in particular about her.

The young woman and doctor did meet once, though, during the first few weeks when the young woman was still new in town. She had heard that the doctor was coming to town and had tried to avoid any encounter with him. She stayed indoors as much as she could. Yet to her surprise, he had come to the widow's door when the widow was not at home, to call on another of the widow's boarders. The young woman had let the doctor in. They spoke quietly in the parlor for a few minutes before the doctor went to the room of the boarder on whom he was calling. When he had finished with the boarder, he let himself out of the widow's house and left immediately for the next town. The young woman had watched him go from the window of her room. She avoided all company for the rest of the day and was not quite her cheerful self for a couple of days following.

2

Another

"See, your king comes to you."

The young woman's pensive mood changed quickly days later with an event that the town expected as little as her own arrival. Another traveler came to town to stay for a while.

The traveler was a young man, nearly a boy in frame but of impressive bearing and character. *He had fine appearance and handsome features.* He bore himself with such confidence that his carriage and upbringing seemed almost aristocratic. While the young woman had entered the town quietly looking for a simple room, the young man made a command entrance. At the town clerk's tiny window, he requested not a boarder's room but a meeting with the mayor. The nonplussed clerk had indicated that the mayor was unavailable just then. In fact, the town had only a ceremonial mayor whose more substantial roles included the town's only street cleaner, law enforcement, firefighter, and undertaker. The young man had thanked the clerk, said that he would wait until the mayor was available, and taken a seat on the bench outside the tiny window.

The young man's innocence amused the clerk. She thought first of explaining to the young man that the mayor, such as he was, would not make much of an audience for the young man. Something else in the young man's demeanor, though, made the clerk think otherwise. *He gives orders and they obey him.* So she slipped out the back door of the tiny town hall to search for the mayor. She did not have to search far. The mayor, dressed in dusty overalls, was leaning on his shovel in the shade up against one of the town's few main-street buildings, in the usual spot where he took rest from his street-cleaning work. The clerk approached.

"You've got a visitor asking the mayor's audience," she found herself saying in bemusement, even to her own surprise.

The mayor snorted in disbelief and did not move from leaning on his shovel.

"No, you really do," the clerk repeated, this time a little irritated at the mayor's insolence, adding, "He's waiting for you."

Even as she said it, the clerk realized how the visitor's request had elevated in some small but significant way the office of the mayor, even if it had not yet motivated the mayor's person. The town had nothing elevated about it, that much was certain. Yet the fact of the town's downward aspirations did not preclude the possibility of its elevation. That realization had been the source of the clerk's irritation with the mayor. *The older men should be worthy of respect.* She had no expectation that he would dress for anyone, distinguished visitor or other, as anything other than the town's general laborer. Yet he still had official duties that he should take seriously.

As she thought of these things, the clerk pulled herself up a little higher, turned toward the town hall, and marched off. The mayor watched her go, at first having no inclination of following. Something in her walk, though, made him reconsider. *They held back until a mother arose.* If a visitor wanted an audience with the mayor, then the visitor should have one, he concluded as he watched the clerk march off. He leaned down to brush a little of the dust off his overalls before following the clerk. The shovel he left leaning against the building, waiting for him to return to finish the day's work.

Symbol of Atonement

The clerk slipped in the town hall's back door. She hoped to watch from her tiny clerk's window the mayor's first encounter with the visitor. The mayor entered by the hall's front door, stomping the dust from his boots on the hair rug inside before coming upon the visitor seated on the hallway bench. The visitor rose from the bench extending his right hand to the mayor in regal fashion. The mayor looked at the extended hand for a moment. Shake it, you lout, the clerk watching from the window wanted to holler. Yet she just watched, wincing at the mayor's awkward pause.

One could understand the mayor's hesitation. The town had not seen handshakes, indeed niceties or formalities of any kind, for a long time. The visitor's extended hand briefly brought the mayor back in memory to a couple of decades earlier when handshakes were common not just between strangers greeting one another for the first time but even among friends and acquaintances. Right then, the mayor resolved to extend his own hand more frequently. Now, he took the visitor's hand in his own and gave it a hearty shake. The visitor smiled warmly at the mayor.

"Your Honor, so good to have your acquaintance," the young man said with warmth equaling his smile.

The mayor smiled back, especially at the honorific that the young man had used to address him. He inquired politely of the young man's name and, having answer, then added, "What can I do for you?"

"My intent is to find lodging befitting my purpose and plans," the young man replied. As he did so, he seemed to look over the mayor's head into a distant future. The mayor started to turn to see where the young man might be looking before realizing the figurative vision.

"And what might those plans be?" the mayor asked, instantly regretting the direct nature of his question, which sounded even to the mayor far too suspicious toward a person of the young man's innocence and stature. So the mayor quickly added, "I mean, so that we might discuss your lodging."

The young man simply replied, "More of that later," indicating neither offense nor condescension. He then looked directly at the mayor, asking, "Would you give me the privilege of a tour of the town?"

"Why certainly," the mayor replied. He looked down at his dusty overalls and boots. He then added something that surprised even himself, saying, "Would you please give me a minute to, uh, compose myself?"

The young man nodded his assent, indicating with a gesture and word that he would wait for the mayor in the shade outside on the town hall's porch. The moment that the young man stepped out through the hall's front door, the mayor ran out the back, making for his little house nearby. Minutes later, the mayor returned dressed in his finest black suit, reserved heretofore for the funerals he conducted.

Word had already begun to spread through the town, in the way that word does in small towns, that it had a distinguished visitor. *News about him spread quickly.* By the time that the mayor and young man embarked on their leisurely walk down the town's main street, residents were peering from windows and standing in front of stores and homes. Mayor and visitor chatted amiably with residents, accompanying every greeting with formal introduction of the type that the visitor had first offered the mayor. Within little more than an hour, everyone in town knew the visitor and his plan, such as it was, to find lodging suitable for his undisclosed intention. *He could not keep his presence secret.*

At that point, the young man asked if he might retire for a bit to catch his breath from his travels and tour, before confirming any plans for lodging. The seamstress offered her sitting room. The town folk, who had formed a parade of sorts following the mayor and visitor on the tour, agreed that the sitting room was most suitable for the rest of such a distinguished guest. The seamstress showed the young man to her sitting room, where she left him to rest.

The young man's temporary absence facilitated a town debate over his most appropriate lodging. The mayor moderated the debate. Strangely, though, the debate did not include the young man's bona fides or intentions. On the couple of occasions when someone asked who the young man was and what he planned for his stay, others quickly cut off the questions. The young man's good character and intentions were obvious from his manner and bearing. They had no need for reassuring information. The only question was where to put up the young man during his undefined stay. *The Son of Man has no place to lay his head.*

With but a few moderating words from the mayor, the assembly quickly reached accord that a room at the widow's house would be beneath the young man's station. The miller proposed one of the summer cottages down by the river. For a moment, the assembly looked as if it would resolve in favor. Then someone — the drugstore clerk later claimed it was her idea — proposed the old mansion at the top of the main street, across from the abandoned church grounds. Initially, the assembly scoffed. The mansion had remained shuttered for years. Yet brief debate revealed that it would take but a few hours to make habitable a single room within it.

The assembly commissioned the mayor to present the mansion's offer to the young man. The mayor returned from the seamstress's sitting room with the young man's gracious acceptance. The news spawned the assembly's impromptu cheer. In their excitement, residents called out spontaneously the actions each would take immediately to reopen the mansion for the young man's use. No moderating, planning, or debate took place. Each resident simply announced their action and headed off to execute it.

An observer might have construed their actions as competition among one another to win the young man's favor. One would have to know their hearts to know their reasons. Without knowing their individual motivation, all would still take it as obvious that the town had not rallied with such unity around any purpose in many years, if ever. The young man's presence had immediate salutary effects on the town's spirit. Something in the condition of the town and character of the young man had brought the town together.

The young man spent the next several days making the mansion more habitable while thanking, getting to know, and further relying on the town's residents who had installed him there so generously. He soon learned that the mansion belonged to a distant benefactor with whom no one in the town had any recent communication. The benefactor had once been so generous to the town and with so many of its residents that the residents all assumed that the benefactor would support this convenient use of his mansion. When the young man learned of the benefactor's title to the property, he resolved publicly to contact the benefactor to investigate the mansion's proper lease or purchase. While none of the residents felt such circumspection to be necessary, it nonetheless further elevated the young man's reputation. If the young man wished to keep his affairs so in order, then the town folk were all behind him.

Barely a week passed before the delivery to the mansion's address of a large envelope. Word spread even of that small eventuality. The following day, the young man confirmed publicly that he had acquired title to the mansion from the benefactor. In doing so, the young man announced his plan to restore the mansion to its former glory, if the town's residents were only willing to lend him their support. *Who remembers this house's former glory?* In return, he offered to lead the restoration of the church grounds across the street from the mansion.

Residents did not immediately accept the young man's offer. Indeed, the offer evoked much quiet dissent. The dissent took two forms. The first was whether the town and its residents should so favor the young man's private interests. Given that he now owned the mansion, they would be helping him improve its condition thereby increasing its value. Why not improve their own homes, they asked? The second reason had to do with the young man's offer to lead the restoration of the church grounds. No one had advocated that restoration. The church stood long abandoned. What need had the town of a restored church grounds?

Epiphany— Star of the Magi

Yet in the face of the young man's evident good character and uplifting demeanor, the town's newfound generosity carried the day. The long-anticipated demise of another of the town's elderly residents, and the brief grave-side memorial the mayor offered, provided the mayor with an odd but fortuitous occasion to poll the town's residents and announce their decision.

"As sad as it is to see another loved one depart," the mayor spoke soberly at graveside, "We have recently welcomed to town a young man whom the departed had also welcomed. The young man has offered to restore our church grounds, if we only help him restore his own residence, which we all recognize as the symbol of the town. All in favor of the young man's offer please indicate by your assent."

The mayor's words brought scattered ayes, growing slowly to a chorus, even as the residents seemed to listen for the reassurance of one another's votes.

"All opposed to the young man's offer please indicate by your nay," the mayor rejoined when the chorus of ayes subsided. His words brought nary a nay, causing him to conclude, "Then be resolved that we move forward in support of the young man's generous plans."

The young man, who had stood respectfully some distance from the graveside, stepped forward to thank each resident, even as he simultaneously offered his condolences for their neighbor's passing. His comforting words and kind gestures reinforced in every resident that they had resolved correctly. No plans were in place, but the residents had made a public commitment. The work would take its shape according to each resident's means. *The glory of this house will be greater than the former house.* The young man and residents left the graveside together, leaving the mayor to finish his undertaker's work.

The first work entailed clearing the mansion grounds of its overgrown bushes and weeds, with which the town's residents happily pitched in. Residents also cheerily contributed plantings from their own gardens to improve the mansion grounds. Nothing warms neighbors' hearts like sharing garden plantings. In a short while, the work transformed the mansion grounds, giving the high end of town an earnest (if not yet entirely kempt) look. *The workers restored the temple.*

The work's first delay came when the residents turned to the mansion itself. The work required lumber, paint, and other supplies. No one including the young man had yet mentioned who would pay for those supplies. At the same time, no one wished to confront the young man over the question. Everyone wished to preserve the fact and appearance of commitment in good faith. The work simply slowed to accommodate the lack. Residents turned to what little remaining clean-up work they could find.

The town's old retired scrivener, who had taken to watching the work each day, noticed the slowing of the work. He caught the young man on his way out of the mansion one day.

"My young friend," the retired scrivener addressed the young man at the street, "Might I have a moment with you?"

"Why certainly, dear sir," the young man replied, adding with a warm smile, "You know that I value your wisdom, drawn from long service in such a noble profession."

The young man placed one hand behind the old scrivener and with the other hand made a gesture back toward the mansion. Together, they went inside, taking seats on small chairs set temporarily by the mansion's largest bay window.

"With what commerce or society may I assist you?" the young man asked the old scrivener, with more than his usual formality, once they had settled and finished polite small talk. The young man had gotten to know and like the scrivener for his thoughtfulness.

"My mission is not to ask but to offer assistance," the scrivener replied with equal formality. "I have noticed the slowing of the work and suspect that its cause might be the question of funds."

The young man took a deep breath to speak, but the scrivener stopped him with the brief motion of a gentle hand toward the young man's knee.

"The benefactor from whom you purchased the mansion would consent to my disclosure," the scrivener resumed. "When he moved from the town now so long ago, he entrusted our small bank with a fund for its upkeep. I do not mean to imply the banker's wrongdoing, but I noticed with sadness over the years that no funds went to the entrusted upkeep."

"My good friend," the young man interjected in protestation, "We have no need of funds here. My hands know the work of carpentry, and the town has already been most generous."

The young man looked to continue, but the scrivener once again interrupted politely.

"I anticipated your kind resistance, my friend, believing wholeheartedly in your good character, generosity, and means," the scrivener continued. "Yet I have already had occasion to speak privately with the banker to whom the benefactor entrusted the funds. That good man now holds open to you an account out of which you may expend such funds as the mansion's restoration requires, so long as no one hears of the source of those funds."

The young man looked down at his hands for the longest moment, breathing slowly and deeply. Tears moistened his eyes when he looked up again at the old scrivener. They rose simultaneously, slowly shaking hands while still looking with respect in one another's eyes. They had nothing more to say between them. Yet just at the door, the scrivener stopped.

"I nearly forgot," the scrivener chuckled. "The funds have grown to the point that they should easily cover the restoration of the church grounds, too. The benefactor's trust also provided for that upkeep."

The young man first smiled broadly at the scrivener and then, as tears began to flow, embraced him in a warm hug of thanks conveyed by action, where words would neither come nor do. Full supply they now had, as is the case with the many good works planned for us. The young man now had only the joyful work to do. *God prepares in advance good works for us to do.*

3

Smitten

"I have walked before you with wholehearted devotion."

While the young woman was well aware of the young man's appearance in town from the constant talk of him, she had yet to encounter him. Indeed, he was so often and so publicly about town, that the young woman must have been studiously avoiding him, or so some thought. She did not discourage the thought and instead lent some fuel to it.

"So what do you think of him?" the widow asked the young woman one afternoon over tea.

"Why, you know I have not met him yet," she replied. "Am I to form opinions of people before meeting them?" she added playfully.

"Of course," the widow rejoined in the same playfulness, "Why wait for a first impression?" They laughed together at her comment.

Yet the widow was not to be distracted, adding, "You might just meet him this evening when he walks the promenade down at the river. You have not been on your own evening walk since he came to town."

The widow eyed the young woman closely for a reaction.

"Yes, I might, and then I might not," the young woman answered coyly, disarming the widow's inveigling. She added with a smile, "Haven't I been getting enough exercise running your errands?"

"What if I send you on an errand to the young man?"

"You and I have no business with him yet, I think," the young woman answered, adding, "The day comes, though, the day comes."

At the same time that she resisted efforts to bring them together, the young woman did not discourage and rather encouraged positive talk of the young man. She also admitted a growing interest in him, even though from afar, as was evident one morning at the baker's shop.

"And what will you and the little friend hiding behind you have this good morning?" The baker smiled at the young woman as he dusted the flour from his hands on his apron.

"Whatever is the freshest treat you have, my dear baker," the young woman replied pertly, adding in response to the baker's jest, "But my invisible little friend must save his treat for the widow."

The baker laughed, the young woman joining him.

"Maybe your invisible little friend should take a treat to the young man's mansion instead of to the widow," the baker ventured, watching the young woman closely for her reaction, just as the widow had done.

"Aye, he should, dear baker," the young woman replied, going along with the game, "Especially if all the good things that I have heard about the young man are true. He sounds a worthy acquaintance."

"He is, he is, my lass," the baker replied, pleased at the young woman's interest. "None understand why you have not yet made his acquaintance. May I do the honor of an introduction?"

"Why, thank you, good baker, but I fear that I must not yet distract him from the wonderful good that he does for so many here."

The young woman let her head fall a little and cast her eyes downward with this last comment, ensuring that the baker understood how deeply she had begun to admire the young man. She then added, "He has changed us, hasn't he?"

The baker did not answer immediately. He put the baked treats in a sack and handed it over the counter to the young woman. Finally, he answered.

"Yes, he has, although I think the change began with you, dear one."

"If in some small way I have prepared a few hearts for him, then in that day may it be to my credit. Yet you speak far too well of me. For all I have heard of the young man, it is too great an honor even to be thought his herald."

The young woman gathered herself to leave. The baker watched her go. As she reached the door of the shop, the baker called to her once more.

"Say, do I hear that you are cleaning the miller's home this afternoon down by the river?"

"Indeed, I am. He and his wife have been most kind to me," the young woman answered.

"Would you mind taking my payment to him then?" the baker asked. His hand brushed the counter once briskly, creating a small cloud of flour, giving him occasion to add with a large smile, "I have continual need of his fine product."

The young woman laughed at the baker's playful gesture, returned to the counter, and took the baker's envelope with the miller's payment.

That afternoon, the young woman met the miller at the mill ground's gate. The miller's dogs bounded back and forth in delight at the young woman's coming. As soon as she entered the gate, the dogs surrounded her, anticipating her hugs and kisses. When the dogs had settled down, the young woman pulled the baker's envelope from her shoulder bag, handing it to the miller.

"Our baker says he wants to ensure that he has more of your fine product," the young woman said as she handed the miller the envelope. The miller looked inside the envelope, using his fingers to count the bills.

"He need not have worried," the miller replied, after a pause adding, "Would you be so kind as to return the envelope and its contents to him for me, please?"

The young woman looked surprised as she accepted the envelope back from the miller. The miller said nothing until they had reached the house.

"Years ago, when my wife took ill, our friend lent me the funds we needed for her treatment. We would have had to sell the mill were it not for his generosity."

"Why do you repay him now?" the young woman asked.

"Oh, quite right, dear one," the miller replied without offense, "I should have done so long ago. I have been telling myself that he did not need it because he never asked repayment. I only realized recently how wrong I was in withholding it."

They stood in silence at the door to the house. Finally, the young woman spoke.

"What made you realize it?"

"I have no doubt of it now that it was the young man who came to town recently," the miller answered.

"What did the young man say or do?"

The miller reflected another moment before answering, "Nothing obvious, I suppose. His good character simply had a gentle way of convicting my conscience."

The miller hung his head. Then he continued.

"I am sorry to involve you in my confession."

The young woman touched the miller's arm in silent reassurance. Just then, the miller's wife opened the house door.

"Why there you two are," she chided them cheerily, adding, "Waiting for an invitation, I suppose."

They all laughed together. The young woman busied herself cleaning for the rest of the afternoon. The miller's wife stopped her briefly at her departure.

"The river is so pretty this time of year, isn't it?" she said as they stood outside the house.

"Yes," the young woman replied, "I find myself spending more time down here as the summer lengthens."

"Perhaps you will come down on Sunday afternoon, then, when the residents gather for refreshment. We've not seen you all summer yet."

"I will," the young woman answered, touching the miller's wife on the arm in parting, and then adding, "I believe that I have an acquaintance to make at the river."

The miller's wife smiled warmly at her, taking her hand and pressing it to her cheek. "So, it is time, is it?"

"Time indeed," the young woman answered. *Who comes to meet me but my master?*

Every resident seemed to be at the river that Sunday afternoon. Many occasionally took their leisure there. Yet word had spread of the long-anticipated meeting, which none would miss. So long had passed since the town had seen one visitor stay, not the less two visitors. That the two visitors would not have met sooner by chance was unusual. That they would meet publicly, at a time that the whole town anticipated, was an event. The town's provincial and isolated character had combined with the odd coincidence of the two visitors to create an event of historic proportion.

Cross Triumphant, the Lord Glorified

As it turned out, the event did not disappoint. The young man took his usual stroll along the river's promenade in his Sunday finest. The weather was perfect. The sky was cloudless. The dry air retained the cool of morning, seeming to be so pure as to shimmer in the brilliant sunlight. The pristine light and air gave radiance to the young man that was even greater than the abundance of his natural vitality and distinction. His clothing seemed to shimmer right along with the air and sun.

The young man passed leisurely down the riverside path. Residents fell quietly in behind him. None knew precisely where or how the two would meet. None would miss it. The man had begun his promenade at one end of the riverside greenway for which outsiders knew the town. That greenway was the one natural object that gave the town some distinction. By the time the young man approached the point at which the town's main street ended at the greenway, his procession had drawn most of the town's residents in his wake.

Despite the procession's size, the young man took no notice of it. His vision was on the brilliant sky, beautiful river, and splendid greenway. As had been his habit on Sunday promenades, he took no particular notice of anyone, certainly engaging no one in idle conversation. Whatever held his attention on these strolls was instead too special. He was to cherish each moment of it. Although none gave voice to the sentiment, the residents recognized his uninterrupted stroll as fitting his kingly character. On this occasion especially, no one dared to impede his regal progress toward meeting the young woman, a meeting that the residents believed he did not expect but would not regret.

Then, they saw her entering the greenway at the end of the main street. The barber, who kept his shop open every Sunday, later said that he saw her come down the main street slowly, like a heavenly vision. She seemed to descend on the greenway more so than enter it. She wore a fluttering summer outfit all in white, stirred into angelic wings by her graceful movement. *The Spirit of God descended like a dove.* No one had seen her dress in anything like it. The young woman had worn everyday clothes, nothing but work clothes really. Yet here she appeared, dressed practically as a poor bride might dress for a small town summer wedding. *His bride has made herself ready.*

Her entry into the greenway halted the young man's procession yet just a little ways off. He regarded her appearance without expression. The processing residents slowly took up positions in a wide circle around him, where they could observe his expression. They later agreed that his demeanor changed not in the least. None said later what they might have expected from him. Perhaps none had thought. The event's anticipation might have been too great for it to admit to speculation about its detail and outcome. One thing was clear, that the young woman's appearance would not alter the young man. His demeanor remained throughout the event as composed and regal as it had before she met him.

The young woman's reaction was the opposite. She had entered the greenway nearly as composed as the young man, even if not nearly so richly appointed. Yet her entire appearance changed the moment that she encountered him. Her path had taken her directly in front of him, where he had stopped to observe her entry. *The Spirit of God alighted on him.* She did not look at him, indeed did not seem to notice him, until she stood directly in front of him. Just then, when she turned facing him, catching for the first time his unwavering gaze, she crumbled. *Your procession, God, has come into view.* Some residents said later that she had made a gasp. Others recalled various audible expressions akin to wonder. Though the residents could not agree on what she had said, they all agreed that she had collapsed on the path in front of the young man.

The wide circle of residents around the young man and young woman at first took alarm at the young woman's collapse. Some prepared to rush to her. Yet at the next moment, the young woman had somehow composed herself into kneeling submission before the young man. Her face was down on the path, her arms outstretched before her with her hands turned up toward the young man. *She bowed down with her face to the ground.* Her posture was so remarkable, so unprecedented, that the residents' alarm turned almost instantly to shock. Her words that followed only confirmed the startled effect on the residents.

"Oh, my Lord," the young woman said, only slowly lifting her face from the path but still not daring to look straight at him, "it is indeed you, about whom I have heard so much and for whom I already have such devotion."

Here, the young woman paused. She remained kneeling but no longer with her face down against the path and instead sitting up, folding her hands across her breast, still keeping her head bowed. *So was the radiance around him.* Her pause gave the wide circle of residents a moment to examine the young man's reaction. He had none. His look remained as impassive and distant as if nothing more than a butterfly had arrested his progress. Yet his silence in no manner deterred the young woman, who resumed.

"Word of you caused my heart to stir as never had it stirred before. Yet now that I look upon you, as little as I dare in your glory, I find my heart forever transformed. Your radiance is a wonder too great to behold. The beauty of your spirit compels me to submit, which I do most willingly, for I have nothing to withhold from one as great as you."

Residents remembered little more of the much else that the young woman spoke. Whenever recalling and discussing it later, they all agreed that she spoke nothing other than to the young man's utter devotion. She was smitten in a manner none had ever witnessed. *I remember the devotion of your youth.* Indeed, each recalled her words having spellbound them. Old and not-so-old, man and woman, rough and refined, each felt enraptured. They could not even recall how long her devotion had held them. The young woman herself finally broke their spell.

"I must away, lest your divine countenance annihilate me," the young woman ended what had been the most unusual of soliloquies. *The Son is the radiance of God's glory.*

She rose from her kneeling position quickly, turned back down the main street, and hastened away like some gossamer apparition. The wide circle of residents parted for her exit but remained otherwise motionless and speechless. They watched her go until she disappeared up the main street. The young man's gaze had also turned to watch the young woman's figure scurrying back up the main street, presumably to her room in the widow's residence. Her departure left the gathered assembly silent, each in his or her own thoughts, like a curtain drawn.

4

Disdain

"Neither cast ye your pearls before swine."

The tanner's wife was the first to speak.

"Well, I have never seen such a preposterously immature display," she muttered just loud enough for several others to hear.

"Embarrassing," the miller's wife added, nodding her head, after a glance around the circle showed no protest to the first comment and instead silent assent.

"More than that, shocking," the seamstress chimed in louder than the others, seeing no disagreement. She then added, "A ridiculous putting on of airs."

"Such abject submission does not befit a person," another woman agreed, adding, "What would be left of our dignity?"

This comment linking the young woman's display with what someone might expect of others struck a chord with several of the gathered women. Within moments, several more women in the circle had agreed. They began talking together in twos and threes. Indeed, an observer might have gotten the sense that the young woman's display had finally given excuse for pent-up feelings to vent. Hardly anyone had spoken a negative word about the young woman since her arrival. Now, negative words sprang forth like weeds in a freshly hoed garden. *Slander springs like poisonous weeds in a plowed field.*

As much as the event excited many of the women in the group, the men in the wide circle remained silent. The men may have been waiting to hear from the young man, from whom they seemed willing to take their cue. Devotion can be a precious commodity. None wanted to criticize it too quickly, even if its full display had left them as shocked as the young woman's display had ruffled many of the women. The young man, though, still did not speak. He seemed particularly pensive, as if he too was trying to come to terms with the extraordinary event. The mayor finally stepped into the vacuum created by the young man's silence.

"It does seem most unbefitting to our customs," the mayor seconded the women who had been speaking with growing clamor. The mayor sent his comment aloft like a trial balloon to see which way the wind might take it.

The women who had been speaking nodded and murmured loudly, indeed almost cheered, in agreement. The men in the wide circle of course noticed the vigor of their affirmative response. In a moment or two, several of the men were nodding, too. Fantasies about devotion were now lost. One of the men recalled offense he had taken at something that the young woman had said. Another man questioned whether she had done as he had once asked. In a few more moments, the circle of residents seemed unanimous in growing disdain for the young woman. In such ways do factions form. *Factions and envy are works of the flesh.*

Then, the young man spoke, interrupting the residents' growing clamor of condemnation.

"I, too, had not expected what we just witnessed," the young man suddenly interjected in a firm voice. The circle grew instantly silent. The young man paused for the longest moment before resuming, just when it seemed someone else would speak.

"How do you mark it, perhaps as a delusion?" he proposed, looking slowly all the way around the circle. *Let you without sin throw the first stone at her.*

No one answered the young man's question. Several residents instead looked down, already feeling ashamed while sensing what was coming.

"If that is your consensus, then my view is that we indulge the young woman until her recovery," the young man said.

Everyone in the circle knew that they had expressed no such consensus. They had condemned the young woman. No one had mentioned delusion.

"Until now," the young man continued, except that he paused at this point to look again around the circle, "I had not heard an ill word of her. If you find reason to question her conduct this afternoon, then let us hope that you find less reason as time passes."

By now, the young man's gaze had fallen, a change that the residents construed correctly as the young man's disappointment, either in them or in the moment. *The sins of slavery will disappoint you.* None had seen the young man disappointed at any moment since his arrival. None wanted to be the first source of it. The moment made the residents restless. Someone had to break the uncomfortable silence. The mayor, knowing his role, did so.

"What, good sir, do you mean by indulging her? Displays of this kind could be most upsetting."

"Yes, I see," the young man acknowledged. He did so with a slight shake of the head indicating that he was only acknowledging, not necessarily agreeing. After another moment's pause, he continued, "Let us hope then that she restricts her displays of, of … ," and here the young man paused, searching for the right word before continuing, "… of fidelity in a way so as to discomfit none other than me."

The young man had enunciated and emphasized his odd word *fidelity* with an arched brow. He had obviously chosen his words carefully. *Words should support those who stumble.* Recognizing his care, the circle of residents contemplated his words before any responded.

"Does she not upset you?" attempted the tanner's wife, who after all had been the first to speak against the young woman's display. She saw clearly that her own reputation would now be at stake, dependent on the young man's judgment. *Have a reputation of being alive, not dead.* Several of the residents smiled, catching the tone of unction that she had given her query. They knew the tanner's wife to be quick and hard to judge, not unctuous.

"My feelings are of less concern than that the young woman regain herself," the young man replied generously.

The nonplused look of the tanner's wife showed that his comment had settled it. What, after all, could they do but continue with relationships as their conduct had established them? The young man was the first to move. He simply resumed his promenade along the greenway, looking for all appearances as if nothing had happened. The mayor was the next to move, following the young man as he had done just before the strange encounter with the young woman. Other residents disbursed to their shops and homes.

Despite the young man's willingness to proceed as if little or nothing had happened, the young woman's conduct that day had in fact changed relationships. Until the fateful event on the greenway, the young woman and young man had maintained close and supportive relationships with many residents of the town. The young man continued to do so. The young woman did not.

Wheat, Grape, and Vine--Christ's Body and Blood

It was hard to say whether the residents or the young woman were more responsible for the change in their relationship. The residents certainly thought differently of her now. Indeed, they thought of her as deluded, just as the young man had supposed for them. Their supposition caused a certain coolness in their relationship toward her. That coolness was evident in every small exchange that followed the greenway scene.

"Two, please," the young woman motioned toward the rolls in the baker's glass case. The baker put two rolls in a small bag without looking up from behind the counter.

"My best to the widow," the baker mumbled as he handed the rolls over the counter and picked up the coin the young woman had placed on the counter.

The young woman curtsied briefly, turned, and left, all without looking up. The baker and the next customer gossiped quietly at the counter, watching the young woman leave.

Later the same day, the young woman met the miller at the gate, picking up a small bag of flour and delivering the widow's payment. The dogs had bounded to the fence, where the young woman leaned over the fence to greet and pet them. She did not open the gate, and the miller did not ask her in. The miller's wife watched their brief exchange from the small home's window.

"We won't be needing any help this week," the schoolteacher told the young woman outside the widow's house that evening. The young woman had been straightening up the schoolroom and even helping some with lessons.

"Thank you, Ma'am," the young woman had said, adding a bit sadly, "Give my best to the dear children."

The schoolteacher almost said something but then did not reply. She just nodded and went on her way down the main street to her usual evening repast, where, imbibing more than usual, she and her companions had good laughs at the young woman's expense. *Share no foolish talk or coarse joking.* As the banker's daughter, the schoolteacher had always had fewer cares than most, contributing to her enjoyable evening repast.

Indeed, the town's residents made no secret among themselves how much less they thought of the young woman since the advent of her strange delusion. She became something of a pariah, even as she continued to make her way on errands around town. *Blessed are you when they exclude you.* They gave her no direct offense, and she took none, instead continuing in every relationship pretty much as she had before the greenway scene. Yet the town had clearly turned against her. She found many fewer opportunities for the cheerful service she had formerly supplied in generous quantities to many residents. Soon, the brook of her light commerce had almost entirely dried up in the withering judgment of the town's residents.

The town's turning would have been surprising but for the character of its residents. The young woman's happy enterprise in the weeks leading up to the greenway event had certainly earned her a measure of grace. Yet the residents, very much in keeping with the town's stodgy character, were unwilling to extend her the grace that she had earned. The greenway scene itself was also no clear reason for the young woman's condemnation. If the residents had treated it as theater, for instance, then they might have applauded not only her eloquence but also the concept her eloquence represented. The men who had witnessed her display had appeared ready to applaud it in some measure, if the women's contrary condemnation had not carried the moment. *Bad company corrupts good character.* The town had much more to accomplish before sustaining a modicum of charity.

The town's turning against the young woman was also clearly not what the young man desired. That afternoon on the greenway, he had not in any direct or indirect manner condemned the young woman's devotion. He had not even indicated that he felt it strange or inappropriate. He had only inferred correctly that the town would not accept it. The town had not done so. The young man had done the best that he could in turning condemnation toward tolerance. *Tolerate me just as you would a fool.* In the days following the event, the residents remained barely cordial toward the young woman. For his part, the young man took pains to make clear his respect for her.

"I am so sorry for your embarrassment this past Sunday," the parson said to the young man as they sat resting one afternoon on the porch of the mansion. They had been repairing wood trim and doing other carpentry work inside.

The parson did not miss the young man's brief startled look at the parson's comment. The parson realized instantly that he had misread the young man in some unexpected way. So before the young man could reply, the parson continued.

"Of course, I assume that the young woman's, well, display must have been one to which you were not, let's say, accustomed."

The parson smiled kindly as he spoke, to be sure that the young man appreciated the parson's effort at sensitivity. The parson did not intend to speak poorly of the young woman, who right then was attending the parson's wife back at the parsonage. The parson realized that he had made the comment more to have something idle to discuss than to make any judgments. *Busybodies say things they ought not to.* The moment caused the parson to recall something from his long-past days of ministry, about the evils of idle talk. His vague recollection increased the uneasiness that the young man's startled look had begun in him.

"Though many here have presumed otherwise, I am in fact familiar with devotion, even devotion well beyond the young woman's brief Sunday display," the young man replied without looking at the parson.

Something in the manner that the young man said these words, and in the young man's far-off look, sent a chill up the parson's spine. The young man seemed not so much to look into the distance but to look back in time—far back in time, more so than the young man's youth permitted. The parson felt gray hairs stand at the back of his old neck. The chill unnerved the parson, whose turn it was now to be startled. The parson vaguely recognized the other-worldly feeling that the young man's words and look had created, although years had passed since he last felt it. The parson's recollection, though, triggered a question rather than a riposte.

"What ought we to make of such devotion?"

Even as he asked it, the parson realized that it was the sort of question that a young man would have asked an elder. *They found him in the temple courts asking questions.* That the parson had asked what we (rather than he) should make of the young woman's devotion made his question all the clearer that he was asking not simply for himself but on behalf of the townsfolk. It had been years since he had in any sense interceded for the town's residents, he realized simultaneously. The parson knew that the young man had a generally positive effect on him, as the young man had on other residents. Yet this influence was something new.

"You are the first to ask the right question, my good parson," the young man smiled back.

The parson instantly recognized that he was once again in the young man's favor. The brief conversation also confirmed for the parson that he valued the young man's favor well beyond their natural relationship as neighbors and growing friends. The parson studied the young man's continuing warm smile. He could see that the young man was not going to answer the parson's question about the young woman's devotion. The parson smiled back at the young man. Then they laughed together at the same instant. *The One enthroned in heaven laughs.* The parson had felt before that he and the young man somehow communicated without speaking. He knew, too, that he and the young man had just laughed precisely because they had silently acknowledged to one another that the parson's question would remain pending.

For her part, the young woman continued in her other-worldly devotion toward the young man. The young man walked the parson back to the parsonage, where they met the parson's wife and the young woman inside in the kitchen. The moment that the young woman set eyes on the young man framed by the kitchen doorway, she dropped her head, beginning to bow deeply in the young man's direction. She was about to kneel when the young man stepped forward and caught her hand. She looked up into his eyes, he down into hers, for the longest of moments. The parson and his wife later agreed that the moment might have lasted minutes, hours, or even years, for all they knew.

The Crucifixion

Eventually, though, the young man spoke, breaking the spell. Later, the parson could not quite get straight just what the young man had said to the young woman. He almost seemed to have spoken to her in a language intended only for the two of them. The parson's wife was of no help in recalling the young man's words. They had the character, though, of the young man having said, "The truth your devotion has revealed to you does not now require your submission."

Whatever the young man had said had satisfied the young woman, who turned quietly back to the kitchen table to pick up her bag. She then made her way gently to the kitchen door. As she passed the young man, she paused just briefly enough to pinch lightly the hem of his coat between her thumb and forefinger. *Who touched my clothes?* Far from incongruous, her simple gesture conveyed the respect of a commoner touching the mantle of royalty.

The parson noticed the young man's hand move as if in benediction. The young woman stepped quickly out. The young man turned again to the parson and his wife, smiling gently. He nodded a gentle farewell, backing out of the kitchen.

The young man had not taken long to answer the parson's question. The parson soon put his wife to bed gently. He then sat at the kitchen table, weeping late into the night.

Residents reported to one another similar encounters between the young man and young woman over the next days and weeks. No resident had the parson's insight into the nature of those encounters. Nor did the encounters produce in any resident the response of the parson. The souls of the other residents must have had more to accomplish than did the parson's. *Break up your unplowed ground.* The residents remained unappreciative of the young woman's conduct, to say the least. Many remained disdainful. Yet their reactions in no sense deterred the young woman. Her devotion to the young man seemed instead if anything to increase. The residents might hardly have thought that increase possible given the young woman's initial displays that to the residents had made her devotion appear total. Yet more than possible, she proved it.

5

Betrothal

"My beloved is mine, and I am his."

The increasing encounters between the young woman and young man, and the young woman's increasing devotion, soon reached a point of crisis. That crisis occurred, though, not because of the young woman's conduct. Rather, it occurred because of her health.

The times between her encounters of the young man steadily decreased. It had taken many days for her to encounter the young man for the first time at the greenway. Several days had passed before she had seen him again at the parsonage. A couple of days more had passed before she had encountered him again at the seamstress's shop. Thereafter, she had seen him daily at various places about town and before too much longer multiple times daily.

To those who followed the encounters between the young man and young woman, which meant most of the town's residents, the encounters seemed natural enough. Commerce among the town's residents had always been fairly frequent. The town's residents had need of one another. In the days and then weeks following the young woman's arrival, that commerce had increased as the young woman had made her way merrily about town helping residents complete their long-overdue errands.

The young man's arrival had further increased interaction among the residents. His work on the mansion had in particular brought together old acquaintances, even helped to settle old scores, as one event well illustrated.

"Ah, look here," the young man asked his friend the barber one Saturday morning as they inspected the much-improved condition of the upstairs rooms, "Do you think that we might obtain some expert counsel regarding the finer appointment of these rooms?" *My father's house has many rooms.*

"What do you mean, sir?" the barber replied as they looked into another of the sunlit upper rooms, "Your taste seems the match for any of our remaining projects."

"My taste is precisely the concern, my good man, that any house that reflects only its master's taste is an inhospitable abode." *I go there to prepare a place for you.*

The barber laughed, clapping the young man on the back as he did so. The young man laughed with him. The barber then suddenly looked serious. He stepped into the sunlit room, making his way to its window. Looking out the window across the rooftops of the town, he spoke again, this time quietly and seriously.

"Forgive me, my friend, but I know just the one to help you with finer appointments. I had not thought of her skill in years."

"So tell me, brother," the young man replied after a respectful pause, matching the barber's seriousness and adding, "Giving confession if you wish to the reason for the passing years."

The barber and young man spent the next few minutes discussing quietly the relationship's break and its unfortunate cause. Soon, the barber straightened, wiped his tears, and spoke more cheerily.

"Well then, I think I will ask the young woman to fetch my former fiancé to you. I am sure that both will enjoy the opportunity to make your company again."

It was the young man's turn to clap the barber on the back. They left the upstairs in quiet but good-natured banter.

The constant commerce made natural the increasing encounters between the young woman and young man. No one had any thought that the young woman might have been pursuing the young man or the young man the young woman. They instead seemed clearly to be trying to go about their days innocent of the pursuit or even thought of one another. Still, their encounters steadily increased in frequency and shortened in interval without any obvious plan. The whole affair had the sense of well-designed theater in which one hardly notices the drama's quickening pace. Tell me where you are working—I love you so much.

The shortening intervals seemed to take ever greater tolls on the young woman. The barber, who had already heard that the young woman was under growing distress, unfortunately witnessed her decline first hand.

"My dear friend," the barber said to the widow at the door to her house, "Would you be so kind as to inquire of the young woman whether she might escort a former acquaintance of mine to the young man's mansion to lend him some decorating advice?"

"Why, yes, I suspect that she might enjoy that errand," the widow replied, "except that she seems to have taken ill precisely over having too few such occasions for the young man's company."

"I had heard that they met often," the barber replied not in contradiction but just reporting fact.

"Oh, they had indeed, more and more so, but not often enough to keep the young woman's health. She has taken to pining for him the moment they are apart and has now worried herself sick."

The two stood at the door in silence for a moment, each in their own thoughts. Why should I be left outside the orbit of your tender care? Then the widow spoke.

"I tell you, let's have a visit with her. Perhaps we can together help her make some sense."

The Spirit Descends

They made their way to the door of the young woman's room where the widow knocked. Hearing the young woman's invitation, they entered. The young woman's appearance shocked the barber. She lay wan in bed, cover pulled to her chin, her face colorless, her eyes without spark. *My bones waste away in my groaning.* She looked away to the window as they entered, saying nothing in greeting. The barber had never seen such a swift decline from youthful good health. Embarrassed at having stared gaping at the young woman's ill health, the barber quickly stammered his invitation.

"Oh, Miss, the young man wishes your help in escorting an expert acquaintance through his rooms for decorating advice."

The barber realized as he finished his request that the young woman had hardly heard him beyond his first words that the young man desired her in some respect.

"He desires me, my acquaintance, my… ," the young woman stammered in a rush, nearly jumping from the bed with a distracted look. *Your desire will be for your husband.* Fully dressed already, she searched frantically for her light coat and bag even as she spoke.

"Yes, Miss, to visit him in the company of my former acquaintance, whose address over by the fields I will share with you."

"I will head to him at once," the young woman replied, quickening her search for her coat.

"No, Miss, I said to the fields to invite and accompany my acquaintance."

"I am not to see him?" the young woman said, freezing in her frantic search while giving the barber a look of bewilderment. In the next moment, she was back in a heap on the bed, sobbing. *Let me see your face, let me hear your voice.*

The widow gave the barber a disgusted look as she moved to the bedside to console the young woman.

"Of course you are to see him, dear," the widow soothed her, "Only you must have reason, which the good barber has just given you. You cannot simply chase after the young man to gaze upon him."

The young woman's sobs stopped. She sat abruptly up on the bed, now staring fiercely at the widow and barber.

"Why have I need of reason?" the young woman asked almost coldly, adding, "My devotion is all I have to offer and must ever be enough."

Her voice, seeming to come from a distance, trailed off as she finished. She simultaneously slumped to the floor, fainting in a heap. The widow was at the young woman's side but not quickly enough to keep the young woman's head from striking the wooden floor with a thump. The barber now had his turn to look back at the widow with irritation. Yet he was also quickly to the young woman's side helping the widow lift her back on the bed. Widow and barber then looked at one another, sharing their disbelief over what had just occurred. The barber spoke first after another moment's pause.

"Her condition is so much worse than I had expected," he said solemnly, even apologetically, adding, "Were she my child, I would be calling the doctor." *Is there no physician there?*

The barber's sensitivity, surprising even himself, injected a needed dose of tenderness in their considerations. Barber and widow briefly discussed the young woman's decline. They realized then that she needed care they were unable to provide. A moment's further reflection led the two to agree that the young woman's condition required the doctor's help. After all, she had struck her head on the floor while fainting. Surely, that injury warranted the doctor's examination.

The doctor would pass through town that evening, they knew. The widow sent her niece to the station master to request the doctor's attendance. By nightfall, he was at the young woman's bedside in quiet consultation. Before too long, the doctor sent the widow's niece to fetch the young man. The young man soon joined the doctor at the young woman's bedside, their consultation lasting late into the evening. The doctor and young man finally departed together for the young man's mansion, where the doctor spent the night. The doctor left town early the next morning on the next train before the town awoke.

Word of these events spread quickly through town, raising speculation to a fevered pitch. What was the young woman's diagnosis? The residents all shared the same thought that the young woman's delusion had simply grown into full-blown psychosis. That conclusion seemed plain enough. The question was not the source and nature of her suffering. Rather, the question was its cure. Who could imagine remedy for what appeared to be incurable devotion? *Turn to me, dear lover.*

The residents had not long to wait for their answer. The young man emerged late morning to visit the parson. Residents saw the young man leave the parsonage only a little while later. His route took him to a destination that no one expected, especially the matron whom he visited.

"Good morning, dear Madam," the young man greeted the matron through the screen door to her emporium. He had rung the bell for her because she kept the place locked. The matron eyed the young man with open suspicion, still holding the inside door she had swung open only partly. She looked as if she might shut the door at any instant.

The matron had been one of the few residents, indeed perhaps the only resident, who had not engaged the young man in happy society since his arrival. No one was surprised. The matron had remained a virtual recluse since her husband had abandoned her years earlier. The residents tolerated the matron's increasingly eccentric secrecy, even paranoia, out of sympathy for its apparent cause. Her husband had reportedly left her for another woman. They never saw him again. The matron kept entirely to herself. She rarely opened the emporium that her husband had once cheerfully run, only to supply a resident with some necessary curative or to sell an item to raise funds for her own bread.

"Good morning, dear Madam," the young man repeated exactly as he had begun a moment before, once he could see the matron's eyes focus clearly on his face. "I have great need of an item that your fine establishment is sure to supply me."

The matron did not reply immediately. From her upstairs window facing the main street, she had seen this young man moving about town. She had surmised correctly that residents regarded him highly. She had also seen the young woman moving about town and knew of her reputation. The matron, though eccentric, had a discerning spirit. She knew what a young man of standing would seek from her emporium in such circumstances. The young man looked steadily at her, as she looked steadily back at the young man. Neither moved; neither spoke. *My King, garlanded for his wedding.*

Then, after the longest moment, she turned swiftly without a word or expression, disappearing once again inside the emporium but leaving the door ajar exactly as she had first opened it. The young man made no move. He simply remained standing silently outside the screen door. A couple of residents passed him on the street, gawking and wondering. Still, the young man made no move. The longest time passed, with only slight sounds from inside as if of a search for something. *Search for hidden treasure.* It might have been minutes or it might have been an hour that the young man stood outside the emporium's door.

Then, almost imperceptibly, the screen door opened—just a little, but it opened. A hand reached slowly out. The young man reached forward to accept what the hand offered. Placing the small offering inconspicuously in his coat pocket, the young man made a small but gracious bow toward the now-closed screen door. His action included a slight movement forward of one hand, giving his bow more the look of benediction. Residents who observed this secretive exchange reported having heard weeping inside the emporium immediately after. *Oh why does the childless woman weep?*

The Symbolic Hand of God

It took little time for the entire town to construe the nature of the odd exchange. The young man headed straight from the emporium to the widow's house, where he called upon the young woman. The widow brought the young woman to the parlor of the old house to meet the young man. To the widow's consternation, the young woman remained completely composed this time, only bowing her head slightly in recognition of the young man. The young man stopped the widow as she turned to leave. Then, turning back to the young woman, the young man reached into his pocket, pulling from it an exquisite engagement ring.

The offer and acceptance were over in an instant. The widow was either too surprised later to recall any of its details, or details there may have been none. The young man had proposed to the young woman, and she had accepted. *You have stolen my heart, my bride.* The young woman turned to hug the widow. The young man accepted the widow's offered hug. He then indicated his intent to see the mayor. The widow dispatched her niece, who had secretly watched the event from the hallway, to fetch the mayor. The widow, young man, and young woman sat in the parlor waiting. The widow could not later remember what they had discussed. Soon, though, they saw through the parlor window the mayor running in their direction. The sight of the mayor's ungainly haste made the three laugh, breaking their solemnity over the momentous occasion.

"Your Honor," the young man greeted the mayor as the widow showed him into the parlor. The young man stepped forward offering his hand and adding without hesitation, "We have the most felicitous occasion of our impending betrothal to announce and celebrate." *A bridegroom rejoices over his bride.*

The mayor would have already known from the word of the widow's niece. Yet to make his intention clear, the young man directed the mayor's attention to the young woman, who stood silent and demure. The mayor simply stared speechless at the young man and young woman. Not wanting to embarrass the mayor in his awkward silence, the young man continued.

"I desired that you be the first to receive and communicate this official word. Now, we must travel to the county seat for the marriage license and the church there for the ceremony, given that the parson's certificate of ordination has lapsed." *Your builder will marry you.*

The mayor still did not move or speak. The widow, giving the mayor an irritated look with which he was familiar, stepped forward again to embrace the young woman and hold the young man's hand. Coming to his senses, the mayor did likewise. The young woman departed for her room to make preparations for the travel. The young man left the widow's house chatting amiably with the mayor, on the way to the mansion likewise to prepare for travel. As soon as the young man reached the mansion and parted the mayor's company, the mayor headed straight down the main street, hoping without much prospect that he would be the first to share the news. *Share news that brings a reward.*

Residents saw the young man and young woman board the train that afternoon for the county seat. Their departure left the residents wide room to speculate.

"Well, think of it," the seamstress told her gathered audience, "The burden on him of her derangement must have been enormous."

Heads nodded assent. The seamstress continued.

"Think of the poor man not being able even to go out without fear of such embarrassing attention. Why, he might just as well have left town for his own good health, doubtless leaving us with the burden of her complete derangement."

The seamstress smiled at the inventiveness of her own imagination, while her audience snickered its approval. The scene thereafter repeated itself all over town, as soon as the audience disbanded. *The wicked spread lies.* So does culture arise and confirm itself from the mouth of one and gossip of many.

Most of the men in town agreed with the seamstress's judgment that in accepting betrothal, the young man had capitulated to the young woman's deranged mind. Their perspective was only slightly different. Several were willing to admit a form of nobility not only in the young man's assent but even in the young woman's derangement. *I delight in my noble ones.*

Those who saw something noble, though, kept their thoughts to themselves. The good sense of few seldom influences the corrupting gossip of many. Indeed, sense spoken to fools can make wise persons targets of the same corrupting gossip. Better is silence among the talk of fools.

6

Marriage

"I will give her to you in marriage; only serve me."

When the young couple returned the next day, presumed if not witnessed betrothed, their relationship with the town's residents necessarily changed once again, just as each of their relationships with the town's residents had changed when young man and young woman first met one another on the greenway. Marriage requires that husband and wife cleave to one another. In so doing, their former relationships must change. If their former relationships did not change, then something would have been imperfect in their presumed union. *They unite to become one flesh.*

For his part, the young man had not changed. Yet because of his union with the young woman, the residents necessarily felt that he could no longer be the secure confidant and good-spirited friend of every resident who wished his company. The residents now had instead to respect that the young woman had gained his confidence in a way that they had not, whether the residents appreciated it or not—and most did not. None disrespected the young man for it, although many disrespected the young woman. Nevertheless, none could be so close to the young man as they had been, at least not until time and experience proved the character of their new relationships. *What God joins, let no one separate.*

For her part, the young woman was no longer the widow's companion. She was even less so the companionable friend of every resident that she had been before she met the young man. She now resided on the second floor of the young man's mansion. In such residence, her devotion to the young man was now perfected and complete. No social convention or physical distance any longer separated her from devotion to the young man. The fire of love stops at nothing. Her commerce with any of the town's residents now depended on the extent to which it promoted the interests of the young man to whom she had committed her full devotion. *She watches over the affairs of her household.*

Yet plenty of opportunity still existed for such commerce. Indeed, those opportunities expanded rather than narrowed through the young woman's commitment to the young man. *Her husband trusts her without reserve.* Looking back on it, that expansion of the residents' relationship with both the young man and young woman would have surprised the residents. Although no one gave voice to it, most would have thought that they were losing both the young woman and young man to one another.

Such loss had been the pattern of love in the town for quite some time. Those who married either left or, if they stayed, in some sense disintegrated into one another. *Is it better not to marry?* The residents likely expected the same to happen here. Anticipating that loss of the young man's good company, not to mention the young woman's service, was likely a cause for the general disdain town folk had for the young woman's winning devotion.

Here, though, the opposite occurred, not so quickly that any resident noticed it, but clearly nonetheless. The young woman's winning devotion to the young man, and the young man's presumed capitulation to it, won for every resident a new source of happy commerce. The positive influence that first the young woman and then the young man had been on the town accelerated with their union. *She dresses for work, eager to get started.* Its beneficial effect proved itself repeatedly in both small and large ways, beginning with the final fitting out of the young couple's mansion.

"I hope that you will consider our offer," the young man concluded, having had no response yet from the befuddled seamstress. The young man gave her a gentlemanly bow but did so without lowering his piercing eyes from the gaze in which he held the seamstress transfixed in her confusion. He then turned and showed himself out of the seamstress's shop.

The young man's generous offer had dumbstruck the seamstress, who from its start had led the quiet insurrection against the young woman's reputation. Indeed, the seamstress's natural venom for anyone whose reputation exceeded her own, when she had little to no reputation, was the reason that the young man's offer had so taken her by surprise. The seamstress expected no favor from the young couple, for she had shown them none.   Yet the young man had just offered her the biggest project—to fashion splendid new curtains for every window in the great mansion—that she would have undertaken in years, if ever. *Give your hungry enemy food to eat.*

The young man's departure brought the seamstress to her wits. She first hurried to the door out of which the young man had just stepped so briskly a moment earlier, hoping by catching a glimpse of him to confirm what already seemed to her like a dream. She saw no sign of the young man but instead noticed an envelope that he had apparently left on the sideboard by the door. The envelope, holding the funds for the entire project, answered a question that had already dawned on the seamstress, which was how she would possibly afford the fine materials that the young man had specified when making his offer. He had advanced the funds. All she need do was to apply her considerable skills in his service.

The Crown of Thorns

One might have thought from the seamstress's venomous character that the envelope of considerable funds would in some other way distort and tempt the seamstress. Instead, the young man's generosity marked by his grand consignment had the opposite effect. The seamstress felt the tight grip of bitterness so deep that she had not even recognized it, dissolve from her spirit. Instantly, she knew, she had lost the impulse for gossip. Her hands would now work in place of her mouth. *Make it your ambition to mind your own business.* Within a week, she took her first sample to the mansion.

"Oh, I had hoped to see your husband," the seamstress told the young woman who greeted her at the door. The seamstress stood awkwardly for a moment on the mansion's porch, gossamer curtains draped gently over her arms.

"Quite alright, my friend," the young woman replied while opening the door further and gesturing the seamstress in, adding, "Come right in and let's take a look."

The seamstress indeed stepped in but did so looking around for the young man's rescue. The seamstress had not intended to deal with the young woman whose reputation she had formerly so scorned. She felt awkward to say the least. Yet the young woman was having none of it.

"Oh, these look simply marvelous," the young woman was already saying as she scooped the light curtains from the seamstress's reluctant arms as they made their way into the parlor. There, she wafted the curtains over the back of a couch like a fisherman tossing a net. The curtains settled gently over the couch. The young woman then began pointing out each fine feature of the work, gradually drawing the seamstress into describing the high quality of her labors and how much time the rest of the work would take.

"I have an idea, then," the young woman finally announced. "The young couple with the twins has fallen on such hard times since the husband's injury while building. Would you work with the young wife who already shows a fine hand for sewing?" *Make it your ambition to work with your hands.*

The seamstress instantly opened her mouth to demur. She had never worked with anyone on her projects. She had never seen work up to her own standards and expected that she never would. Yet just as quickly as she began to decline, something made her hesitate and then, to her surprise, agree to the request. "Of course," she heard herself saying, feeling quite as if someone had taken over her body, "I would love to involve so earnest and needful of a young mother in my lonely work."

"Well, then, it's settled," the young woman beamed back at the seamstress, taking both of her hands in her own just as the young man entered the parlor.

"So, you've settled it already without me," the young man laughed at the two of them still holding hands. Letting go of the seamstress's hands and taking the young man's hands instead, the young woman replied cheerily about the curtains' high quality and the seamstress's gracious willingness to involve the young mother in the rest of the work. *How handsome you are, my beloved!* The seamstress, though, did not miss the young man's double meaning, that she and the young woman had also put aside their differences over the young woman's conduct and reputation. Something in the young man's look let the seamstress know that he had intended both meanings. *Go reconcile with your sister, then offer your gift.*

While the new wife attended to the mansion's fitting, the young man turned his attention to the derelict church. The young man quickly became a close acquaintance of the wizened old man who ran the saw mill well downstream from the miller's grist works. The church needed much work, beginning with replacing some beams and timbers, and much siding and floorboards. The young man spent hours down at the saw mill, returning with heavy boards in hand and covered with sawdust. *All hard work brings a profit.* He also brought back sad news of the old man's loss.

"His son left many years ago, taking with him much of my dear friend's small fortune," the young man explained to his new bride one midday as he rested on the mansion's porch from his saw-mill labors. "News of his son's swift bankruptcy soon reached my friend, who grieves for his now-destitute and aimless son." *He squandered his wealth in wild living.* The young man quietly brushed sawdust from his pants.

"Does he not know of his father's love for him?" the young woman asked.

"Aye, he knows, he knows. Yet though the father long ago forgave him, he has yet to forgive himself."

The two could see the doctor walking up the street toward the mansion. Their gaze turned from the doctor to one another. They slowly smiled at one another. The young woman spoke first, saying only, "Go and do the work you must, my husband."

The young man rose from his seat on the porch to hale the doctor. A moment's talk at curbside brought the young man back to the porch, where the young woman already had his traveling bag ready for him. They embraced briefly before he was off with the doctor toward the train station. No words passed between them when the young man returned late the next day. His wife knew to trust him. *We are messengers, errand runners for the Son.*

Early the next week, two young men walked up the street. Though both laden with heavy boards, they conversed brightly, laughing and gesturing as their loads permitted. In candor, few town folk were surprised that the old man's son had returned to help his father at the saw mill. Indeed, they had so long expected the event that it hardly seemed unusual. The town folk had not expected a series of events that accompanied it.

"You have heard the happy news of my son's return," the old man was telling another of the town's several shopkeepers. "Please then give him my full credit for anything he asks of you," the old man added.

The old man's last words left the shopkeeper speechless, like others with whom the old man had spoken. Each had known the son's reputation for extravagance. While each had expected the destitute son's necessary return, none had expected the old man to once again stand behind the son's credit. Prudence would have dictated the opposite course, not to let the son once again waste the hard-won fruits of the father's considerable saw-mill labors. Yet they also each felt that something undefinable had changed in the son, even if nothing had changed in the steadfast father.

The young man's marriage to the young woman had equally deep effect in repairing other relationships.

"So good to see you and your dusty locks, my friend," the barber chided the young man as he eased back into the barber's chair and the barber tossed his light sheet over the young man's dusty clothes. "You are still hard at work down at the saw mill, I see."

"No work is hard when for the Father's house," the young man smiled back at the barber, although the young man's weariness as he settled deeply into the chair and closed his eyes confirmed the considerable physical effort that the church work entailed.

"Aye, your progress all can see—and all appreciate," the barber rejoined, then added, "Perhaps the news of my impending marriage will cheer you in your labors."

The barber had tried to make the announcement seem business-as-usual, like the small talk in which barbers engage patrons as they perform their kind service. Yet the young man would have none of it. He immediately rose, tossing aside the barber's sheet in order to embrace the barber heartily. The barber, still holding scissors and comb, wiped his eyes with the back of his hand when the long embrace was over.

"You are to be our honored luncheon guest then," the young man said grandly with a flourish of his hand toward the shop door, "Let my bride and our day's friends share your joy."

The barber held up scissors and comb in protest, but the young man only added, "Another time, another time," clapping the barber on the shoulder to turn him toward the door for the short walk to the mansion luncheon. *He made the water into wine.* No one had planned it, but the barber and his fiancé ended up celebrating for the entire afternoon at the mansion. Guests came and went freely while all in attendance shared stories of married bliss and more than a little innocent mischief.

The Mother's Pierced Heart

The union of young man and young woman now ensconced happily in the mansion had broader effect than simply healing old relationships. Their presence and influence also stimulated new relationships.

"My strong young friend," the young man was saying to the sawmill owner's son one day as they rested from their labors repairing the last of the benches in the church's sanctuary, "On last Sunday's walk, my wife and I so enjoyed your company and that of the schoolteacher with whom you seem to spend more and more time."

The young man's friend looked down at his callused hands for a moment before replying, "May I have your advice, good friend?"

Minutes later, the town's residents saw the young man and his friend heading down to the sawmill. Prying minds could tell that something was afoot. Events late that day added to suspicions, especially when the town clerk saw the schoolteacher and parson leaving the young couple's mansion. The sawmill owner's son had also briefly visited the matron's emporium.

Barely a night passed before the town's residents knew of the happy couple's engagement. No announcement was necessary, the news instead having traveled as news always did in the small town, from mouth to ear, more swiftly than any possible technology.

The engagement of the sawmill owner's son to the banker's daughter proved more than any other single event the valuable commerce that had flowed through the town with the coming and then the marriage of the young man and young woman. The sawmill owner promptly engaged the scrivener to prepare a deed for a parcel of his sawmill lands on which the new couple would construct their marital home. The sawmill owner simultaneously retained the twin's father, who was gradually recovering from his injury, to plan the home's construction. The twin's father would work with the baker's toothless customer who, most had forgotten, had once himself been a skilled tradesman. The sawmill owner's largesse was primarily possible because of the funds he had earned from supplying the lumber for the reconstruction of church and mansion.

Not to be outdone, the banker promptly retained the dry goods store owner to order the new home's necessary household goods, the seamstress to work on the new home's finer appointments, and the tanner to provide leathers for the couple's carriage, tack, and seating. The dry goods store owner was even able to put her disabled husband to work on the orders.

It was certainly unusual to the town to see such blessings flow from ordinary engagements like that of the barber and his fiancé or the sawmill owner's son and the schoolteacher. Yet first the character of the young woman and young man, and especially then their betrothal and marriage, had changed things. Their marriage had multiplied their happy influence on everything. *It yielded a crop a hundred times more than sown.*

~

7

Ministry

"Will not the Spirit's ministry be even more glorious?"

Of course, marriage requires a ceremony, and a ceremony needs a place to perform it.

Fortunately, the young man and townsfolk were just completing the church. Indeed, the young man and parson had already begun quietly holding times of prayer, worship, and communion in the old building's sanctuary. They had made no announcement of service times or days. They had not even discussed doing so. Together, they had simply discerned that private prayer, worship, and communion were necessary to restore the vitality of what had once been a vibrant body. *Do not give up meeting together to encourage one another.*

The parson drew much strength and wisdom from these private times. The young man's few words of prayer and worship reached deep inside the pastor, informing not so much his mind as the Great Spirit still living within him. The pastor discovered that faith itself had not grown cold, only that he had for a season looked away from it. He had grown cold while faith burned and brightened just as intensely as always. *The love of most will grow cold.*

The pastor also learned of his responsibility to facilitate and restore corporate worship and connection. We are incomplete when not belonging to one another in the right sense of belonging, the pastor now knew. We cannot live isolated, on islands. Our identity forms in its greatest part by interaction with, indeed in loving service to, others. *Live out your God-created identity generously toward others.* This truth the parson had long known. He had only recently discovered its corporate dimension.

The Altar of Burnt Offering

The town's languor the parson had long attributed to its innate somnolent character or perhaps to the backward character of a few of its more-notorious denizens. *Cretans are liars and lazy gluttons.* Yet the parson now realized that the town need not have taken any such peculiarly negative character, if it had only retained the Great Spirit who had once enlivened it, just as the town now once again received that spirit.

The parson was also realizing the inestimable power of the young man's words on the few occasions when he spoke in earnest. *He explained what scripture said concerning himself.* The event that the parson most recalled occurred when several others had joined the parson and young man in the sanctuary early one Sunday morning. Several had made a loose practice of stopping by the sanctuary early on Sunday. Yet on this occasion, all had coincidentally stopped by at once, giving the young man, who was always in attendance, more of an audience than usual.

The parson could not say later that the young man had actually preached. Rather, all that the parson could recall is that the young man had spoken many words that instructed deeply. *Were not our hearts burning while he talked?* Others who had attended, including the barber and sawmill owner's son, had later shared the same impression. All had left the church that morning feeling as if the young man's words had changed them forever, shaped them into someone new who they had not been previously. Each had already respected the young man deeply. Yet each had later shared how startled they were that the young man's words had such transformative power. *They were not able to recognize who he was.*

The marriages of barber to fiancé and sawmill owner's son to schoolteacher were thus the first times when the whole community once again used the restored church. Both weddings were of course festive affairs. *Come to the wedding banquet.* Each wedding seemed to remove from the town the tarnish of old ways and older wounds. The parson presided over both weddings. Everyone later said how vital the parson had seemed, not at all dour as they remembered him before the church had shuttered.

Indeed, the weddings served the dual purpose of reestablishing the church body and order. Informal boards and committees had to form simply to pull off the two ceremonies. Those happy organs soon served as formal corporate structures within the newly formed church. *Do everything in fitting order.* Before long, the town seemed once again to revolve around Wednesday evening and Sunday morning services, just as it had done so long before.

The young woman played a critical if unusual role in the church's regeneration. She took no formal role, instead remaining a sort of outsider to the busy work of the townsfolk many of whom reconstituted their old roles within the new church. The young woman instead continued to focus her intense devotion on the young man but now in a way that simultaneously served and invigorated the church.

"Have you seen the love with which he regards the town's children?" the young woman was asking the barber's new wife one day as they relaxed in the cool of the mansion's parlor.

The barber's wife had grown accustomed to the odd way that the young woman seemed to live, nearly breathless, through the young man's preferences. Unlike most of the town's residents, though, the barber's wife had no objection to the young woman's extraordinary devotion. She had instead recognized instantly how reliable were the young man's preferences and how peculiarly insightful the young woman was at reading them.

"What might you have in mind?" the barber's wife replied simply with a knowing smile.

"Well, what if we were to begin a day care at the church, that the children might have more frequent occasion to delight him?" the young woman replied.

"Has the town such a need?" the barber's wife rejoined, for a moment forgetting her companion's devotion. The young woman seemed not to hear the barber's wife, who had already realized her error in even asking. Instead, the barber's wife tried again.

"Do you think he would like that?"

"Oh, I am sure he would," the young woman almost squealed in delight. Anyone else would have thought the young woman to be nearly senseless or at the least naïve in the extreme, but again the barber's wife knew better.

"How shall we begin, then?" the barber's wife asked, with no further debate, indeed, with no consideration given at all, to the merits or possibility of the young woman's proposal. Whatever pleased the young man, the young woman would do, the barber's wife knew and somehow subtly trusted.

Within weeks, children filled the church's small activities room each weekday morning. The young woman, barber's wife, and tanner's wife took turns caring for the children, while the young man indeed stopped by often. Each time he did, children overwhelmed him, pulling at his leg until he scooped one of them up and continuing to clamor about him until he would sit and then roll on the floor with them. *Let the little children come to me.*

While nothing had demonstrated the town's need for a daycare, the fact of its establishment had other happy consequences beyond the young man's delight. Residents had initially scoffed at the daycare's announcement. Several parents who had enrolled children did so out of pity for the young woman more so than need.

Yet beyond the parents' newfound freedom to work or accomplish other tasks, the parents' interaction with the daycare's tiny staff and with one another as they delivered and fetched their children had its own salutary effect. Parents got to know one another, sharing support, resources, and tips. Parents and their children also began to frequent other church activities including prayer and worship.

One of these interactions sparked the young woman's next project in pursuit of the young man's satisfaction.

"Where has your good wife been lately?" the young woman asked a father as he dropped off his infant daughter, adding, "The drugstore cannot have kept her these long hours."

"Sick, lassie—I mean ma'am," the father replied, momentarily forgetting the young woman's still-recent marriage. "The drugstore hasn't seen hide or hair of her either." The father handed his infant daughter to the young woman.

"Oh dear," the young woman replied as she took the child from the father's arms, adding to herself, "He would be most concerned for her healing."

"Pardon, ma'am?" the father asked as he stepped back from handing over his daughter.

"Healing means so much to him," the young woman continued, again more to herself than in response to the father's question, as she bounced the child on her hip and smiled down at the child.

"To whom?" the father asked again quizzically.

"Certainly, we could do more to please him," the young woman continued almost wistfully, still not acknowledging the father's questions and instead still staring and smiling at the infant in her arms.

"Well, um, have a good day, ma'am, and I'll be back to pick up my dear one," the father said as he backed out the door.

"Wave to papa," the young woman said to the man's infant daughter who instead smiled up at her as the father backed out of the door waving. Neither the young woman nor the infant looked up at him.

Late that same day the town's residents noticed the doctor leaving the mansion. No one had seen the doctor arrive in town. Everyone soon learned the purpose of his visit. Early the following day a parish nurse arrived, taking a room at the widow's home. The widow's word traveled swiftly through town. The young woman and doctor had arranged for the nurse to care for the sick drugstore clerk. Beyond that care, the nurse would remain as long as anyone else in the town needed her. *He sent them to heal the sick.*

The drugstore clerk healed fairly quickly under the nurse's expert care, though they agreed that her recovery was a feat that she would not have accomplished nearly so quickly, if at all, without that care.

The Annunciation's Purity

Yet the parish nurse stayed on. The town's residents could find her at the church office every day when she was not making visits around town. Her visits often took her above the dry goods store where she worked with the owner's disabled husband.

Before long, townsfolk were astonished to see the owner's husband making his way slowly down the street aided only now and then by the nurse. *The healthy need no doctor, only the sick.* Years had passed since his last public appearance. The store's owner and her disabled husband were soon able to occupy a bench together in the church sanctuary at the opposite end of town. Customers also found the husband at light work in the store.

The nurse also kept busy visiting the twins' injured father whose slow recovery had stalled without a full return to work. The father had kept busy leading the construction of the new home of the sawmill owner's son and his wife. With the nurse's skilled therapies, the father was able to do some of the actual construction rather than just direct it, restoring his hope for a full recovery.

The nurse also often visited the shut-in emporium matron. No one knew what therapy or counsel the nurse might have provided the matron, who remained reclusive. Yet some residents claimed to see evidence of the emporium's restoration—especially that things had moved about the interior, which seemed less dusty and dark.

The men who had helped repair the mansion and church also continued their carpentry work as a ministry adjunct to the church. The parson, not the young woman, had proposed this service work. The parson knew from his own carpentry work of the unfilled needs of various poorer townsfolk for such items as bed frames, work tables, and repaired gates. While each of the men who participated had their own daily work to complete, together they found extra time to help the parson take on these odd volunteer projects. *Each gave according to his ability.*

Like the daycare and parish nurse's work, the carpentry ministry seemed to lift the town from its listlessness. Those gains were in part the effect of many small improvements in the lives of the town's poorer residents. Providing a new bed for a growing child or work table for the homemaker, or fixing a broken gate, lifts a home's spirits. Yet service work also lifts spirits in the homes of the servers. *It is more blessed to give than to receive.* Nearly everywhere one looked, the town seemed to have lifted its spirits.

One exception stood out among the residents' growing good cheer. With his every visit, mostly unannounced, the doctor retained his somber spirit. Residents tried to cheer him up. They joked with him and even teased him, expecting him at some point to return their good humor. The doctor seemed especially dour when they called his attention to the church and its several programs, or to the mansion and its young residents.

"You must stop by the mansion to encourage our leading young couple," the mayor entreated the doctor on one of his surprise visits, adding, "You hardly have an idea of all that they have done."

"Ideas I have plenty," the doctor scowled back, concluding, "Yet none that would serve."

"Here now," the mayor rejoined, "We have no need for dark thoughts on such a cheerful day. I have seen you attend to the young couple's needs promptly and without objection. Why not give them due encouragement?"

The doctor neither replied nor looked at the mayor. Instead, he turned his head to look off into the distance, as if he might be hearing a call for help from a distant town.

Then, just as the mayor began to speak again, the doctor announced abruptly, "Good day," and strode off toward the train station.

The mayor put his hands on his hips and huffed disapprovingly. He then turned the opposite way toward the mansion to do as he had urged the doctor to do, which was to encourage the leading young couple.

~

8

Malady

"Will I recover from this illness?"

The mayor found the young couple at home in the mansion but not in the good straits he had expected. The young man and young woman had, since their marriage, always been in good health and spirits on every public appearance or private visit. This day, though, was different.

"Greetings, my good friend," the mayor had haled the young man at the mansion's door, expecting the young man's characteristic heartfelt hug, slap on the back, and warm welcome.

Instead, the young man looked respectfully back at the mayor and, while still holding the door ajar, said simply, "Ah, Your Honor, my apologies, but I must attend to my bride's indisposition." The door then closed, leaving the mayor outside.

The young man's few words and closed door nonplussed the mayor, who stood in shock like a statue. His mouth may have hung open if he had even had the sense about him to recognize it, so surprisingly uncharacteristic was the young man's cursory greeting.

No one knows how long the mayor might have stood on the mansion's porch but for the parish nurse's sudden arrival.

"Excuse me," the parish nurse said without further greeting. She pushed her way brusquely past the sentinel mayor, opened the door, stepped in, and closed the door behind her.

The parish nurse's nearly impudent action in virtually ignoring the mayor was too much for him to take. He was not a turnstile. The nurse's arrival had turned his curiosity over the young woman's alleged indisposition into alarm over what might be her condition. Yet the mayor had no recourse to entering the mansion. Nor could he remain standing on the porch. So he instead made straight for the town's main street to try to learn what his keen antennae must have missed about the young woman's condition.

The town's residents soon learned and shared with one another that the young woman had indeed taken ill. Few actually saw the young woman. Those who did manage to visit her briefly in her upstairs bedroom in the mansion described her as pale and weakening. Most, though, depended on the parish nurse for reports of the young woman's waning health. The nurse was generous in those reports, particularly in that she sought to investigate among the town's residents possible causes for the young woman's illness.

"Had you seen her swimming in the ponds or river?" the nurse asked the dry goods store owner at the store's counter, adding, "Talk in other towns is that the swimming holes are carrying a bad infection this summer."

"No, that would not be like her at all," came the reply, the owner adding a moment later, "But have you replaced the home's earthenware, from which she may be drawing poisons?"

"Why no, hadn't thought of it. Let's just do that, shall we?"

The nurse and dry goods owner busied themselves at picking out new earthenware for the mansion.

"Would you please have it run up to us right this afternoon?" the nurse asked in parting, adding, "No sense in waiting another minute for my poor young charge. She suffers so in her illness."

"You'll find it there before you, my dear," the owner replied. She touched the back of the nurse's hand on the counter while saying, "Now you take good care of our missus."

The nurse stopped at the drugstore on her way back to the mansion, where she greeted the clerk.

"Have you more of that poultice, dear one?" the nurse asked after having given a brief report on the young woman's continued decline.

"Why yes, but if you see no progress yet, then you should really also try a vapor rub," the clerk replied, adding, "I have seen it do wonders for the body and spirit."

"Oh, that would be just the thing to ease her suffering," the nurse replied.

The clerk fetched the products from the deep shelves and slid them across the wide counter. The nurse placed them in her large upholstered bag.

"I have seen much suffering," the nurse said in parting, "but this illness seems darker somehow."

The clerk nodded, adding, "All we can do then is comfort her while hoping that it passes quickly."

Strangely, the doctor made no appearance during the young woman's extended decline. Instead, the parish nurse attended to her, appearing to the townsfolk's satisfaction to provide every possible remedy. Indeed, the parish nurse's diligence and thoroughness discouraged the residents from even thinking of haling the doctor.

"Have you thought it might be stale air coming up from the lagoon at night?" the seamstress asked the nurse as they sipped tea while sitting on a shaded bench in the afternoon heat just outside the baker's shop.

"Why yes, that could be just it," the nurse replied. "I have been sure to shut her window at night, but now I see that I must move her to another room on the other side of the house, perhaps on the lower floor."

The two finished their tea discussing the many ailments and remedies they had seen, and not-few demises they had witnessed in their many years.

Even as the parish nurse made her way about town investigating and collecting remedies for the young woman's strange malady, the young man was uncharacteristically absent. His absence unsettled the town's male residents as much as the young woman's illness unsettled the women.

"Has he not been by your place either?" the sawmill owner asked the miller as they sat one evening down by the river, watching the water birds fish and float by.

"Haven't seen the young man since his wife took ill," the miller replied, adding, "My wife saw him briefly when she visited the young woman, but he said hardly a word to her."

"Not sure what to make of it," the sawmill owner rejoined. "Hardly seems like him to cut us all off even while seeming to ignore her peril."

Indeed, the young man's stand-offish response to the young woman's deep illness engendered in the town's residents a new and unfamiliar attitude toward him.

"What do you make of his few words?" the town clerk asked the mayor after the young man left. The young man had stopped by the town hall to post a letter. He had hardly greeted the mayor and clerk, giving only a shrug, shake of the head, and "can't tell" response to their inquiries over his wife's health.

"Nearly heartless, one might think," the mayor replied.

The clerk nodded in agreement.

Roman Lantern Symbolizing Betrayal

As much as the young man's diffident response to the young woman's extended decline consternated the townsfolk and turned them against him, the young woman's dire circumstance drew the townsfolk to her. The few who were able to see her always found her confident even if suffering severely in steep decline. The young woman's courage in the face of her seeming demise served only to accelerate the residents' regained attraction to her. They thought all the more of her as stories of her courage and of the young man's indifference spread.

The church was the one place that seemed least negatively affected by the young woman's illness and the young man's curious absence. Indeed, the opposite was true, that church attendance rose and programs strengthened notwithstanding their absence. The parson preached with greater vigor than ever. A choir had taken shape, while the barber played his trumpet, and the twins' father a fiddle. The toothless tradesman sometimes accompanied them with anything at hand, whether a washboard, cowbell, or spoons.

The barber's wife ran the daycare, and the parish nurse continued to make her other rounds even while caring for the young woman. The men were more active than ever in their volunteer woodwork. They had even undertaken repairs to benches, fences, signs, and gates in the public spaces around town. Their work had been so evident and effective that talk was of building a hospital and orphanage if they could locate and acquire suitable grounds. The town's residents simply forged ahead in their energetic plans in the absence of the young man and young woman.

The parson played a greater role in the town residents' newfound resolve than he might have known or admitted. His effect was greatest when interpreting in eternal terms the courage that the young woman displayed throughout her extended illness. No doubt, he had to address her condition. The many who now attended church gatherings had resumed the ancient practice of corporate prayer for the ailing. In her severe illness, the young woman was first on the minds of many, after their own family members. The pastor kept the church praying earnestly and often for her comfort and recovery.

Yet the pastor's message went well beyond temporal illness and earthly demise or recovery. The pastor was quick to admit that all suffer eventual demise. *Death is the fate of all humankind.* The unnatural timing of the young woman's decline simply highlighted humankind's shared conundrum. To deal properly with one's anticipated demise requires a right view of the eternal, the pastor advocated. The pastor communicated confidence to his listeners that the young woman held that right view. Some things are true. Others are not. The young woman knew truth and embraced him. *The Lord sustains them on their sickbed.*

Those few residents who had managed to see the young woman in her illness seconded the pastor's observation of her clarity and courage. The parish nurse and young man had been reluctant to allow visitors both because of the young woman's weakness and the uncertain cause and nature of her illness. Those who did visit came away not so much saddened by the young woman's poor condition as heartened by her attitude toward it. Despite her struggle to fight the unknown disease, she seemed, they reported, to look forward to her eternal departure rather than to dread it. *What must I do to inherit eternal life?*

"A step nearer him, always a step nearer," each visitor reported the young woman as having said whenever their brief conversations had reached the unwanted question of her demise or recovery.

In these visits, each guest recognized and reported that the young woman's devotion no longer centered on the young man, her putative husband. Rather, they all reported that her full attention seemed directed beyond her current life to richer life that she anticipated with growing relish. *Whoever believes shall not perish but have eternal life.*

The parson more than managed to communicate her hope in the eternal to all those congregants who heard his messages. He seemed enlivened by her hope, oddly blessed even by her illness. The parson transmitted his vitality to the congregation. In the end, her decline seemed as natural and hopeful as if she were well and engaging in new mission. Death did not sully but rather uplifted her reputation, spreading ever wider her salutary effect on the town's appreciative residents. *Where, O death, is your victory?*

9

Memorial

"Surely the righteous will be remembered forever."

"I had anticipated need of your sensitive services," the young man was telling the mayor in the mansion's parlor, "but my friend the tradesman made the necessary conveyance to the train early this morning, facilitating her rest at a distant but preferred cemetery."

The mayor looked disconsolate for the longest moment before finally summoning his thoughts. "Then what plans have you for a memorial?"

Here, the young man turned to the parson, saying, "I should like to share more of her life and inspiration, and perhaps even to further somewhat her last wishes, at a gathering at the church tomorrow evening."

"Certainly," the parson answered gently, adding, "Exactly as you plan."

"Well, I'll see that the choir meets beforehand," the mayor interjected busily, sensing that the young man and parson were ignoring him. He continued quickly so as not to be interrupted, "And then of course, after the parson speaks, ..."

At this point, though, the parson raised a hand to stop the mayor. The mayor, surprised at the firmness of the parson's gesture, let his voice trail off in mid-sentence. The parson did not even look at the mayor but instead again addressed the young man.

"The forum is yours, and I am yours to command."

At these words, the parson rose to take his leave and, in doing so, motioned toward the mayor in a way that clearly communicated that the mayor was to leave with him. The young man also rose but stood erect at his seat with a far-off look.

The speechless mayor looked back and forth from one figure to the other. Neither figure, though, showed either the slightest uncertainty or slightest interest in recognizing the mayor. The young man was clearly of a mind to which the parson, whether he knew that mind or not, had just as clearly assented. The mayor had nothing to do but to follow the parson as the parson turned for the door. *They do whatever he commands.* They left together, the young man still not having moved from where he stood before his seat or having changed his far-off expression.

An elderly looking woman, heavily cloaked and averting eyes from anyone who might catch her vision, was the last one to squeeze into the last bench seat at the very back of the church the next evening. Every able-bodied resident had squeezed into the church. So many residents were present that few took any notice of the strange cloaked woman, old-appearing but spritely in movement and fully attentive to the proceeding.

The young man finally rose from his seat on the front bench after a long silence had fallen on the assembled crowd. As he stepped forward and then turned, his steady gaze fell first on the back benches where the cloaked woman sat among hushed youth and other late-arrivers. He then addressed the mayor and parson who sat opposite one another on each side of the front row.

"Good sirs," the young man began and then, looking up from the mayor and parson to the packed church, continued, "Indeed, good friends all. You are here to celebrate the life yet so short of the young woman to whom I was still so recently betrothed."

The crowd seemed to settle in with the young man's first words, as crowds do at gatherings where they expect to hear things of import but know that the telling will take some time. The young man indeed had time to take over the things he would tell the residents of the young woman's background and aspirations.

Gethsemane's Agony

"You knew little of her upbringing, of which I now have a few things to tell." The young man continued, "For you will hardly understand the actions she recommended to me that I fully intend to carry out unless you also know some little of her experience and motivation."

Few words other than these could possibly have done more to gain every hearer's fullest attention. Nearly every resident had at one time or another speculated about the young woman's background, some with greater relish and less fairly than others. Evidently, they were now all about to hear the accuracy of their many speculations. *Advance God's work rather than speculate.*

Yet the young man had also referred in his brief introduction to certain actions he planned to take, on the nature and import of which the residents now had no opportunity to speculate. The young man held surprises in mind, no doubt. Whether good, bad, or indifferent, the residents could not tell. All that they could do now was to listen, enraptured. The young man's introduction had, if possible, deepened the already-deep silence into something profound.

Anyone who has frequented crowds knows these moments. Theater, political gatherings, and even sporting events have the design to produce them. The difference that deepened the suspense here was that every resident understood the event's solemnity to be authentic rather than contrived and artificial. Oratory, drama, or close competition were completely unnecessary. The young man could have given a poor performance but still fulfilled the event's strange promise.

Yet the young man did not disappoint in his demeanor any more than in the content of what he conveyed. The residents by now knew the young man well, expecting and even welcoming his poise especially on such a serious occasion. Given the residents' familiarity with the young man, none were surprised that he would speak with command and composure. Yet again given their familiarity with the young man, only a stranger breaking in on the gathering would have recognized the young man's speaking skill as that of a highly trained professional.

"My beloved and I actually shared an unusual personal history, raised not by any parents whom we knew but instead by a traveling troupe of such considerable note that we performed almost solely in the largest cities."

The young man's disclosure set some residents to whispering with one another, as if keeping score on their speculations. He took no notice of the whispers but instead continued.

"Our troupe's success must have been what kept any of you from recognizing either one of us. We never approached such a remote region as this one, which in the end granted us the anonymity that most attracted us to you."

Some in the crowd seemed ready to take strong exception to this turn in the young man's account. Murmurs arose that the young couple might have played the residents as provincial rubes or, worse yet, fools. Yet before these murmurs could take wing into shouted objections, the young man continued with greater voice and command than ever.

"Our motives, though, were genuine. The two of us had long tired of entertaining, even if our particular form of entertainment was dramatic rather than frivolous or scandalous. We wanted our work to have more-lasting impact of the sort that we imagined could only occur by living for an extended time in a single town."

These words stopped the murmuring, restoring to some degree the residents' trust that the young man would not embarrass them. The young man knew that when gathered together, people are quick to defend collectively their own place. The residents once again listened in silence as the young man continued.

"Our challenge, though, was that we had no meaningful service, indeed no gift, to offer any town other than our ability to draw the most out of our own roles and the roles of those around us."

The young man's words finally congealed the seamstress's interruption. She stood from her bench in the third row, gesturing angrily in the young man's direction while interjecting, "Why this playing-acting then is nothing less than a swindle you have perpetrated on us."

The seamstress's bitter words flung at the young man stirred vigorous agreement from several of the residents who rose to stand with the seamstress. The young man let the noisy energy build against him for a few moments before continuing. He seemed not to mind, indeed instead to anticipate and welcome, the objections.

"Why not at all," the young man smiled confidently back at the crowd without looking directly at the seamstress or any of her fellow objectors. He turned now instead to the barber and his wife seated in the second row, seeming to address them individually rather than to address the restless crowd.

"Each of you had taken up roles long before either of us set foot here. Indeed, we each found our work among you to be much easier than we had expected, given our familiarity with those roles, so like the roles we had played and seen others fill in every other city or town we had visited."

The young man then moved swiftly on, sensing the residents' growing impatience.

"Our work here was in any case not acting," the young man said now with less command and greater humility, adding, "While our whole lives from infancy on had been performing, we were finally acting ourselves more than we had ever had such opportunity."

The young man's confession seemed to regain the residents' trust once again. He gave the crowd no chance to reconsider but instead again spoke swiftly, now with greater conviction.

"You see, among the troupe's members, the young woman and I were the only devoted followers of the great King of Kings whose love has so graciously and so recently revived you. As we traveled from city to city, we grieved together over the shuttered churches we found, where the city's residents had lost relationship with the King. We were also devoted from our first memory to the thought and care of one another, although the troupe's strict rules forbade any relationship approaching marriage."

Here, the young man paused, moving one hand to his chin as if for the first time to turn his gaze inward. His actions had the purpose and effect of causing the residents to consider more carefully and to more fully digest what he had just disclosed. He and the young woman had long loved one another and the great King, yet until coming to their town had little opportunity to show it. He then lifted his head as if in realization, then to resume.

The Lion of Judah

"Our every action here simply fulfilled our lifelong commitment to our King and to one another," the young man announced, now regaining his full command and confidence. "Our every word and action was as real as our lifelong practice of the dramatic arts would permit it to be. I had no less love for my Lord, for her, and for you than I at all times exhibited, while she had no less love for us and for you than she displayed."

Here, the young man paused again, longer than silence could sustain, as he very likely intended. The mayor felt it to be his moment, still not appreciating the young man's skill in inducing the mayor to rise and parry. The mayor began somewhat less than respectfully.

"What then have we to do with your love for your King and one another? You need not have involved us."

The mayor's question and remark at first engendered appreciative murmurs. The mayor knew his people even if he did not know the young man quite as well as he suspected.

"Ah, yes," the young man welcomed the mayor's rejoinder, "Quite so that we need not have chosen you in this town. We could just as well have chosen any other. As I have already said, we found the needs of this town to be so much like the needs of every other. Yet I ask, what need have you?"

At these words, the mayor huffed dramatically. He turned away from the young man, speaking directly now to the crowd, "He says *we* have needs, when all that we did was support *him*."

The mayor's remark garnered agreement from nearly all quarters, so strong that it appeared that the memorial might end in favor of an inquisition. The voices of several rose over a growing din, with talk of the hard labor many had provided in support of the young couple. *Some sneered, while others wanted to hear more.* The young man, though, appeared to remain in complete control. The young man waited to speak until just before the throng looked like it might break up the memorial.

"Here, then, is how my betrothed wished to serve you," the young man nearly shouted over the crowd. His mention of the young woman hushed them. The young man continued.

"You speak of things you have done for us, and indeed, you have done much, just as we had need of them. Yet in honor and recognition of your anticipated service, even before you supplied it, we had decided what we now do, which is to deed the mansion and everything in it, indeed everything that we own, back to you in trust for use as hospital and orphanage. I retain no material benefit from your many labors, only the great benefit of having received and shared in your service."

The young man's announcement momentarily stunned the residents, whose silence persisted only briefly. Smiles quickly appeared, followed by hugs, slaps on the back, handshakes, and all other manner of self-congratulation. The mayor and a few others, who had been standing, sat. The young man moved on, cutting short the celebration.

"Let us recognize, though, that the benefit of our common labor goes well beyond anything so temporary as buildings, gates, benches, and fences." Here, the young man looked again at the sawmill owner sitting with his son and his son's schoolteacher wife, and then again at the barber and his wife, the twins' father, and the dry goods store owner and her recovering husband, before continuing.

"Restoring the health and capacity of its residents, and restoring relationships among them, means so much more to a community than restoring use of derelict buildings."

Here the young man paused to enjoy the knowing smiles of so many of the residents. Seatmates on the benches leaned into, smiled at, and hugged one another. The young man then let his gaze rise until he was looking over the heads of the residents once again with that far-off look so familiar to those who knew him. He then completed the memorial.

"Your greatest accomplishment, though, lies not even in these important relationships. My beloved would want nothing other than to remind every one of us that restoring relationship with the King is all that matters, for all other good things must flow from that relationship, one that she at this moment enjoys more richly than any of us. Your gathering again regularly in this place to learn more of and celebrate him is all the evidence that we need that you are yourselves fulfilling your every need through him." *Have Jesus's mindset in your relationship with everyone.*

The young man let these words settle over the congregation for a respectful moment before adding, "I appreciate your attention. Has anyone any remaining concern, comment, or objection?"

No one dared stir.

The Lord as Alpha and Omega

The young man turned to the parson, who rose, asking, "Do you have any news of your own plans, then? I and others here will miss you deeply."

"My dear one," the young man replied using a phrase that none had heard and none but the parson and his wife expected, "While I must start a new life where the memory of my departed bride weighs less heavy, you must know that I will always be with you." *I will give an everlasting name that will endure forever.*

With these final words, the young man walked briskly from the sanctuary, looking at no one. At the young man's last words, the cloaked figure on the last bench rose quickly and slipped out the back of the church.

The memorial had held so much suspense and such surprises that no one was in a hurry to follow either the young man or cloaked woman. Indeed, the mayor held forth, already addressing the questions of the governance of the hospital and orphanage. Others claimed that they had felt at times that they did recognize either the young man or young woman, likely from their having seen such troupes as the young man described perform in distant cities. Others simply celebrated their restored relationships, giving long hugs to new brides, while still others regaled one another with the good cheer that comes from effective service work.

Not a few, though, celebrated inwardly their greatest accomplishment in regaining relationship with the young woman's King. Late that night at their homes, many prayed and wept joyfully in that celebration. The young man and young woman having done much planting, and the Spirit having made the crop grow, the parson now had a rich crop to tend and harvest. The town had abundant spiritual resources on which to draw for generations.

An hour after the young man had finished and left the sanctuary, residents who still lingered outside the church heard the train's whistle. Minutes later, they saw the parson walking back from the train station, having seen off the young man.

Epilogue

No resident ever saw or heard of the young man again.

The hospital took shape quickly despite the young man's departure and the town's loss of his friendship, leadership, and energy. The parish nurse helped, but the traveling doctor was the one who made the greatest difference in the hospital's success. The doctor became the hospital's leading director, as (the residents learned from the parson) the young man had intended. The doctor soon even made the town his permanent residence. To their surprise, residents noticed a great change in the doctor's demeanor. Gone was the dark and secretive mood. In its place, the doctor exhibited something much closer to youthful joy, a transformation none had seen and few imagined possible.

Townsfolk often spoke of the young man and young woman in the doctor's presence. The young couple were after all the hospital's great benefactors and thus the doctor's benefactors as well. The doctor listened to their testimonies politely but had little to say about either the young man or young woman. They were the one subject on which he retained his former secretiveness. A few residents even tried questioning the doctor closely regarding the young woman's illness, but of this questioning he would have nothing to do.

The orphanage took longer to establish. The miller's wife, barber's wife, and seamstress all had much to do with it, while the banker and scrivener provided through the town's distant benefactor for its funding. The orphanage's greatest promoter, though, was the emporium matron, whom the orphans' deep needs finally drew out of her seclusion. In time, the mansion assumed its role as a warm home for many orphans, not a few of whom townsfolk gladly adopted.

Descent from the Cross

While no news of the young man ever reached the town's residents, years after his departure the train's conductor shared an observation among a select few that brought those few special comfort. The conductor told that an old cloaked woman had boarded that train the whistle of which the residents had heard after the young woman's memorial—the same train that the young man then boarded moments later.

The conductor then told that only a young man and young woman left the train at its distant destination, which was another small town much like the one that the young man and old woman had departed. The conductor never told the name of that second town, but legend grew of a devoted young couple whose love for one another and their incomparable King set old lives newly afire in town after town throughout that great region.

Quotation Citations

A cheerful heart is good medicine. Proverbs 17:22.

A bridegroom rejoices over his bride. Isaiah 62:5.

A gossip separates close friends. Proverbs 16:28.

A happy heart makes the face cheerful. Proverbs 15:13.

A trustworthy person keeps a secret. Proverbs 11:13.

Advance God's work rather than speculate. 1 Timothy 1:4.

All hard work brings a profit. Proverbs 14:23.

Bad company corrupts good character. 1 Corinthians 15:33.

Blessed are you when they exclude you. Luke 6:22.

Break up your unplowed ground. Hosea 10:12.

Busybodies say things they ought not to. 1 Timothy 5:13.

Come to the wedding banquet. Matthew 22:4.

Cretans are liars and lazy gluttons. Titus 1:12.

Death is the fate of all humankind. Numbers 16:29.

Do everything in fitting order. 1 Corinthians 14:40.

Do not give up meeting together to encourage one another. Hebrews 10:25.

Each gave according to his ability. Ezra 2:69.

Factions and envy are works of the flesh. Galatians 5:20.

Give your hungry enemy food to eat.   Proverbs 25:21.

Go reconcile with your sister, then offer your gift. Matthew 5:24.

God loves a cheerful giver. 2 Corinthians 9:7.

God prepares in advance good works for us to do. Ephesians 2:10.

Have a reputation of being alive, not dead. Revelation 3:1.

Have Jesus's mindset in your relationship with everyone. Philippians 2:5.

He could not keep his presence secret. Mark 7:24.

He explained what scripture said concerning himself. Luke 24:27.

He made the water into wine. John 4:46.

He sent them to heal the sick. Luke 9:2.

He squandered his wealth in wild living. Luke 15:13.

Her husband trusts her without reserve. Proverbs 31:11.

His bride has made herself ready. Revelation 19:7.

How handsome you are, my beloved! Song of Songs 1:16.

I am a foreigner and stranger among you. Genesis 23:4.

I delight in my noble ones. Psalm 16:3.

I go there to prepare a place for you. John 14:2.

I have walked before you with wholehearted devotion. Isaiah 38:3.

I held him and would not let him go. Song of Songs 3:4.

I remember the devotion of your youth. Jeremiah 2:2.

I was a stranger and you invited me in. Matthew 25:35.

I was hungry and you gave me something to eat. Matthew 25:35.

I will give an everlasting name that will endure forever. Isaiah 56:5.

I will give her to you in marriage; only serve me. 1 Samuel 18:17.

I will give you riches stored in secret places. Isaiah 45:3.

Sins Washed

I will perpetuate your memory through all generations. Psalm 45:17.

If your gift is mercy, do it cheerfully. Romans 12:8.

Is it better not to marry? Matthew 19:10.

Is there no physician there? Jeremiah 8:22.

Isn't this the carpenter? Mark 6:3.

It is more blessed to give than to receive. Acts 20:35.

It yielded a crop a hundred times more than sown. Luke 8:8.

Let the little children come to me. Matthew 19:14.

Let you without sin throw the first stone at her. John 8:7.

Live out your God-created identity generously toward others. Matthew 5:48.

Make it your ambition to mind your own business. 1 Thessalonians 4:11.

Make it your ambition to work with your hands. 1 Thessalonians 4:11.

My beloved is mine, and I am his. Song of Songs 2:16.

My bones waste away in my groaning. Psalm 32:3.

My father's house has many rooms. John 14:2.

Neither cast ye your pearls before swine. Matthew 7:6.

News about him spread quickly. Mark 1:28.

Oh why does the childless woman weep? 1 Samuel 1:8.

Past troubles will hide from my eyes. Isaiah 65:16.

Search for hidden treasure. Proverbs 2:4.

See, your king comes to you. Zechariah 9:9.

Share news that brings a reward. 2 Samuel 18:22.

Share no foolish talk or coarse joking. Ephesians 5:4.

She bowed down with her face to the ground. 1 Samuel 25:23.

She dresses for work, eager to get started. Proverbs 31:15.

She found no room at the inn. Luke 2:7.

She pretended to be insane in their presence. 1 Samuel 21:13.

She sought her God and worked wholeheartedly. 2 Chronicles 31:21.

She stayed and worked with them. Acts 18:3.

She watches over the affairs of her household. Proverbs 31:27.

Slander springs like poisonous weeds in a plowed field. Hosea 10:4.

So was the radiance around him. Ezekiel 1:28.

Some sneered, while others wanted to hear more. Acts 17:32.

Surely the righteous will be remembered forever. Psalm 112:6.

The cheerful heart has a continual feast. Proverbs 15:15.

The city streets will fill with girls playing there. Zechariah 8:5.

The glory of this house will be greater than the former house. Haggai 2:9.

The healthy need no doctor, only the sick. Luke 5:31.

The king's mission was urgent. 1 Samuel 21:8.

The Lord sustains them on their sickbed. Psalm 41:3.

The love of most will grow cold. Matthew 24:12.

The older men should be worthy of respect. Titus 2:2.

The One enthroned in heaven laughs. Psalm 2:4.

The sins of slavery will disappoint you. Jeremiah 2:36.

The Son is the radiance of God's glory. Hebrews 1:3.

The Son of Man has no place to lay his head. Luke 9:58.

The Spirit of God alighted on him. Matthew 3:16.

The Spirit of God descended like a dove. Matthew 3:16.

The wicked spread lies. Psalm 58:3.

The workers restored the temple. 2 Chronicles 34:10.

They do whatever he commands. Job 37:12.

They found him in the temple courts asking questions. Luke 2:46.

They unite to become one flesh. Genesis 2:24.

They were not able to recognize who he was. Luke 24:16.

To your offspring I will give this land. Genesis 12:7.

Tolerate me just as you would a fool. 2 Corinthians 11:16.

We are messengers, errand runners for the Son. 2 Corinthians 4:5.

Were not our hearts burning while he talked? Luke 24:32.

What God joins, let no one separate. Matthew 19:6.

What must I do to inherit eternal life? Mark 10:17.

Where, O death, is your victory? 1 Corinthians 15:55.

Who comes to meet me but my master? Genesis 24:65.

Who remembers this house's former glory? Haggai 2:3.

Who touched my clothes? Mark 5:30.

Whoever believes shall not perish but have eternal life. John 3:16.

Will I recover from this illness? 2 Kings 8:8.

Will not the Spirit's ministry be even more glorious? 2 Corinthians 3:8.

Words should support those who stumble. Job 4:4.

You have stolen my heart, my bride. Song of Songs 4:9.

You must have honest weights and measures. Deuteronomy 25:15.

Your builder will marry you. Isaiah 62:5.

Your desire will be for your husband. Genesis 3:16.

Your procession, God, has come into view. Psalm 68:24.